Unfurled

a novel

Michelle Bailat-Jones

PUBLISHING

New York, NY

Printed in the United States of America.
10 9 8 7 6 5 4 3 2 1

Ig Publishing
Box 2547
New York, NY 10163

www.igpub.com

ISBN: 978-1-632460-75-2 (paperback)

To Emiline

1

NEITHER OF US REALIZED WE'D BEEN living in a borderland all that time, a place where the rules are too often unspoken, never declared. We didn't understand there were passports and checkpoints involved. And that not all three of us would make it through.

"Look!" she'd always said, her fingers tight on my chin.

I always looked. People? Cars? Animals? For a long time I thought this was a game, so I would scan and stare and squint and try. Hoping for a prize, or thinking there was some way to win. But she was always pulling me away before I could figure out what she'd wanted me to see. I never fought her grip on my wrist. I followed her into our car, waited for her to screech us away back to the house. I followed her around corners, and into building alcoves, away from crowds and down side streets. I followed her wherever she led me. I thought this would be enough.

In borderlands the rules often change. Quickly and without warning. We didn't realize this, neither of us, until it was too late.

Until my dad said, "We'll just be running this schooner on our own and that's all there is to it."

And I said, "I know how to furl the sails, Captain."

"You know," he said, "we've been lightering all this time, haven't we? And then she had to start running a chute on us."

I knew what he meant. I knew we'd tacked into a dog-hole and that it would be hard to get back out again. But I also knew we'd have to accept the weight of the cargo that had dropped onto the deck, line it and stack it, secure it as best we could and then set sail for calm waters. We knew to watch for rocks, we knew to get as far away as possible from the cliffs once the boat was riding low with her cargo. The open ocean was After. That's when we both knew we'd made it through. Knew we should never ever look back.

2

I CAN SMELL THE WATER WHEN I OPEN THE BACK door, but there's no salt in it. No kelp or sand or fish. I know there can't be, but I still pull deep, hoping for it, and breathe out my disappointment which flips in my stomach like a roll of nausea. Nothing but river water and the scent of iced-over mud on this side of the Cascades. Then I'm tripping over my boots and swearing because I'm angry at the Knemeyer's for calling me out to their farm like this, at 5 am and into the winter ice. An emergency that is entirely their own fault. I want to tell them to deal with it themselves, turn myself around and climb back upstairs and into bed with Neil. Roll into the sleeping length of him, find his shoulder and settle myself there. Steady and warm. Mornings with Neil are the safest I've ever known and we are only a few years in; I cannot get enough of them. Instead, I zip his old fleece under my work coat, bite down hard on the prickly mountain air and hurry to the car. Trapp slinks along behind me as usual, jumps into the seat beside me. When I've gotten out of town and I'm hugging the curves of Canyon Road, I call my dad to stave off the bad start to my day, knowing he'll be up now and standing with his coffee at the terminal, ready to get on the boat.

"How's the water?"

"Smooth as steel. And there were five fat beautiful harbor seals off Alki." His voice changes, there's laughter in it. "Neil mention the jet skiers from yesterday?"

"He did. Were they divers? In January?"

"Wake riders, I think. Although they moved off quickly enough."

"So you didn't hit any?"

"Sadly, only two." He chuckles and then, "But what species are you up so early for?"

The words fly from my mouth before I can stop them. "Someone who should know better has gone and bred an unstable bitch. There's a problem with the puppies and now I have to clean up the mess."

There is a hard silence, a trap I've opened, but I try to cover it with, "Ugh, don't mind me, it's early, and it's freezing out here."

My dad's pause continues just a beat longer until he says, "Sounds awful. But maybe it won't be as bad as you think."

I talk fast. "I hope so, I hope so. You're right. I'm just pissed off. People make these bad decisions and aren't willing to do the right thing. Now I have to do it and it's no way to start the day."

A quiet sigh reaches me. "Go easy on them. No one's perfect." As he says it, I see him in the wheelhouse of the boat to Bremerton, the rising sun at his back, the dark lip of water and the line of the mountains in his eyes.

"I'm almost there," I say, "I'll call you later."

He tells me to have a good day, and then it's my turn for a long deep breath, "Clear seas, Captain, watch out for whales."

When he says goodbye I'm relieved because there is a smile in his voice again.

Caitlin Knemeyer is waiting for me at the top of the long driveway. She isn't the kind of woman to get flustered but her hands are shaking.

"We got her separated from them," she says as I roll down my window.

"Show me."

I leave Trapp in the car and he barks as we cross the front orchard. We walk fast in the dark and I match my long stride to Caitlin's shorter one, stepping where she steps. The earth is hard and the air slices at my throat. Stepping between two bare walnut trees, another roll of nausea hits me and this time I pause on it, curious. But I step through it, shake my head over it. I should have eaten something, even this early in the morning.

"In here," she says. We turn off the meadow toward the old calving room and I drop my bag because there she is in one of the old stalls, the partitioned door open at the top. Despite it all, she's still so beautiful and I have to admit that I can see why they did it. But now she's a mess and my anger sharpens to a list of calculated observations. The smell of blood and feces, of dog sweat. The sound of raspy breathing. There is blood on her muzzle and a puppy hanging from her jaws. How long has it been hanging there? Has she punctured the skin of its neck? Is it even alive? Her teats are distended and red. The skin of her right foreleg is raw, bitten to the bone. She's pacing—or really just turning herself in a wide circle, the space is so small—the puppy swinging under her chin. I'm not sure she even knows it's in her mouth.

"I warned you," I say. "And you've waited too long to call me."

"I know, I know." Caitlin's face is grim. "Nathaniel can be so stubborn. He—"

I cut her off with a glance because I'm angry with both of them. This dog should not have been bred.

"How many were there?"

"Seven. She killed two right away trying to remove their placentas. We didn't see …"

I imagine they had trouble during the birth. I imagine they realized what would happen just a bit too late. When the dog was already contracting, when she snapped at them if they tried to get near her, and then after, when she started taking it out on the puppies. Just wanting to make her space clean again. I imagine they thought she'd figure it out, that some maternal instinct would kick in if they helped. But instead, she got worse. They always do.

"There are three still in there with her," Caitlin says.

Now I know why her hands are shaking. Is it the money? I quell the uncharitable thought. Caitlin and Nathaniel have been good breeders until now.

"You've called me out here to sedate her?" I ask, because we have to have this conversation.

Caitlin bites her lip. "What is your recommendation?"

"If I can calm her down and get her out of this, then heal that leg, can you keep her?"

"You're asking me if I think we can keep her with our other dogs?"

I nod. We both know how much work would be involved along with some measure of danger for the healthy dogs. Will she be stable again? Caitlin answers me with downturned eyes and the sharp line of her mouth. So I say, "Ok, can you find her a home?"

She doesn't answer me. Her brow furrows. I know she's thinking about her reliability as a breeder. Can they explain what happened, honestly, and give the dog a new home? Hoping she'll go back to normal once the hormones are gone. Hoping there would be no repercussions on their business. I know she won't hand the dog over to the Humane Society. This city is too small and people would talk. Slowly, she shakes her head.

Before the gesture is finished, I'm already gloving up with my bite sleeve and grabbing my syringes. The quicker, the better. "Can anyone get near her?" Caitlin shakes her head. I turn my attention to the dog. There is the puppy in her mouth and another lying against the back wall like a stuffed toy. I don't see a third. Maybe she's eaten it in the time it took Caitlin to meet me outside.

I open the latch to the partition door but hold it closed in front of me. At the sound of the latch, the dog half-skitters at the door but retreats, more focused on her leg. She's far too tired. What I don't understand is why Nathaniel didn't shoot the dog when it all went wrong. That's maybe Caitlin's fault and I've seen it so many times. People don't want to take the responsibility, but you cannot be soft in these situations. Then everyone gets hurt. They might have saved the puppies.

Her movement has shifted her position and that's when we see the third pup. It scoots out from behind her, nuzzling along the lower back leg. Probably she hasn't let any of them suckle, which is why her teats look so painful. She can't lie flat on the floor and she doesn't understand why. If she flips on her side, the puppies are after her so she's probably been on her feet for three solid days, unable to eat, unable to sleep. I warned them she wasn't stable enough to breed. Fucking beautiful dog. A stunning mouse gray with sea-green eyes. Elegantly built. The Knemeyer's have been breeding Weimerainers since Nathaniel's great grandfather settled in Wenatchee. He should have known better. No matter how hard they trained her, she never settled. Never accepted a job well done. Always needed more. Always too busy. A dog that could never find quiet. Hysterical when happy, aggressive when startled. She would never whelp well and I knew this.

The puppy is moving away from her; this is my chance. I inch myself into the room, making very little noise, banking on her inconsistency, her focus on the discomfort of her body. A good dog perceiving the threat would be protecting the puppies already. But she's lost track of me. She's too busy worrying her leg, biting and gnawing because now the pain is giving her something to do.

It's only when I'm all the way inside that she notices me. She's all ripples and teeth and battening down but in a lazy distracted sort of way. Her eyes are unnerving. The green almost human. I keep perfectly still, and we watch each other. I hold my hand behind me, hiding it, my fist clenched tight. This is when I tilt, a lightning fast shift of frame. I tilt away from this room and into another where there's no blood and no dog, where I'm little and I'm trying to get my hand free from the tight grip on it. The hand clamped on mine is so strong. Fingers crushing fingers and I'm squirming in that kitchen chair, coughing on a strand of hair that's fallen into my mouth, and I don't want to but I have to start begging to the eyes focused on me, trying not to cry, *let go, please*, I'm saying, in my politest voice, but the grip just gets tighter and the eyes more intense and I know it's going to be another of the awful things and all I can do is close my own eyes and wait for it. I blink hard to re-shift the frame, blink and blink and blink myself back to this calving room, and then I'm reaching forward as the dog is lunging at me, still too slow, stepping on a puppy as she jumps, and I'm shoving my gloved hand into her mouth as she clamps it on me and then my right hand toward her neck, needle first. Hard, burying a part of the syringe in the muscle.

Her jaw isn't strong enough to break my finger bones; she's much too tired. But it still hurts like hell, and I yell out. Sloppy and horrible, I push the needle deeper into her neck, but it doesn't need to be a clean injection. It just needs to stop her. We tussle and Caitlin is yelling and I feel the syringe break off inside her muscle tissue, but it's already had an effect, her body is slowing even further, her jaw losing its steel. And then she's off of me and it's easy to take the second syringe and get her neatly this time, gently pushing the puppy out of the way, to Caitlin who has come in and is reaching already to save what can be saved.

"Done," I say. And I buckle down onto the floor and let the beautiful dog collapse across my legs. I stroke her as her eyes roll up and close and she shudders gently to her death, and I ignore Caitlin's hemming and nervous chatter. Poor dog. Poor beautiful demented creature. When she is finally still, I reach across and pull the skin of her lips back down from her frozen snarl so she looks sane again.

Two of the puppies are still alive but very weak, so there is no time to think of anything else. Once we get them cleaned up and fed, Caitlin and I bring them to the whelping box at the back of the building where the other puppies are sleeping and warm. Nathaniel is there, feeding the pups and my anger returns. "That's a hell of a way to wake up," I snap, and then, "Do you want me to take her body?"

He keeps his back to me, says thank you in barely a whisper. He is ashamed and I hear my dad again, reminding me not to be so hard on them. I clench my teeth and start again, say I'm sorry he lost the dog. He apologizes to me, a hard rock of sorrow in his voice. It's what I needed to hear, simple as that, and we work side by side while I check through all the other puppies. We have saved four of the original seven. When I leave an hour later, laying the dog's carcass in a blanket in the back, shushing Trapp's nervous whining, there is the satisfaction of numbers. It feels small against the ruthlessness of the dam's death, but it's there nonetheless. I drive back to town and to the clinic through the cold January sunlight.

The anger-sad catches me a mile past the empty Johnson farm and I pull off into their driveway and barely have the car in park in time. There's no one around here so I put some noise into it, wiping the tears as they fall and feeling the pinch in my abdomen where the sorrow sits tight and contained. Trapp noses my shoulder and I lean into his shaggy flank until I'm ok again, the spike of emotion flattening out into calmer waters. I reach for a tissue packet inside Neil's fleece. I bury my nose into the smell of him. Relax. This is my frame—today, my life now—and the other one can no longer affect me. I promise myself to call my dad later tonight, remind him that we're coming to see him at the weekend.

It only takes another fifteen minutes to get to the clinic and in the parking lot my phone beeps with a text from Neil: *This is a lost owl bulletin. How did I miss her?*

I smile and answer: *dawn flight, silent wings.*

And then he's sending me a picture of our kitchen table with only one place setting, one cup of coffee, one glass of orange juice. I send him back a photo of a tree along the river that the morning sun has set on fire.

Caroline is waiting for me at reception and the look on her face tells me that the evaluation rooms are filled and I will have no time to do anything but begin the work of the day. This suits me fine. I grab a muffin from the small clinic kitchen and it settles my stomach. The hours pass with animals and animal owners and I'm pleased there are no more emergencies, just solvable problems: a pair of injured tabby cats, a steady stream of check-ups and vaccinations, and, just before lunch, my favorite Wolfhound with a nasty gash on its metacarpal pad.

In the afternoon, I go about my rounds at the dog and cat kennels and I take extra time with the Jones's alpaca. I've almost completely forgotten about the morning, about the death and the tilt and Nathaniel Knemeyer's shamed apology, but I should know better. A hell of a way to start the day, I said to Nathaniel. But it seems the morning will have nothing on the evening because after Mrs. McCune's Abyssinian and the

Belmont's flat-coat retriever, after three rabbits and one undernourished hamster, Neil walks into the clinic.

He is supposed to be at work. Today is a normal day. And on a normal day we will meet up again at supper and go over our workdays, watch TV or see friends. Today we are supposed to meet Sarah and Harris at 7:00 PM, but here he is instead, Caroline at his side, walking in to where I'm consulting a new client about her breeding cockatiels. He comes in so quickly that he scares the birds and they flap up, a riot of yellow and gray feathers. They land on their owner's head as Neil reaches me and tries to wrap his arms around me. But I pull back because it's on his face already. The thing that's brought him in here at the wrong time of day. I turn away from it; I check the clock. 4:00 PM. Neil should be out in the forest with a group of students right now. He should be out identifying ferns or pinecones, or whatever it is they're studying this time of year. And I know I'm right because there's a horsetail fern sticking up out of his jacket pocket. I know this is a gift for me, and I know he's forgotten it even if he's brought a hand up to bat it away from his chin. I also know this isn't what's brought him in here.

His face is already saying it, but he says it anyway.

"Your father," he says.

I refuse it. I shake my head, shake my whole body against whatever he's saying. The expression on his face and those two words are not a match. I think of only one thing—that I can smell the forest on Neil's jacket. I love this smell almost as much as I love the smell of the ocean. Almost. So I know I must look at Neil's face again, and let myself hear what he's come in to say.

3

"I DON'T WANT THAT," I TELL THE POLICEWOMAN, shoving the plastic bag toward her. It is seven hours later and we're at the hospital in Seattle. Neil is standing behind me so close that the front of his shoes are touching the backs of mine, so close that when I flinch backward from this bag his chin grazes the top of my head. She tries again and this time I fold my arms, stick my hands tight into my armpits. I don't want this. This plastic bag of everything my dad was carrying on his person at the time of the accident. The woman keeps calling them "Mr. Tomlinson's personal belongings" but she's stretching out that last word so all I hear is the word "long" and I think, yes, what could be taking him so long?

We are in an office—a woman brought us in here, specifically came to where we were sitting for a long time in a waiting room and asked us to come into this private office, and Neil and I both pretended we didn't know what this would mean; we walked calmly, side by side, he may have stretched an arm out to me, but only lightly, while he kept a step behind. They gave us their information and we answered their questions: no, we did not require an autopsy; no, my dad did not wear a wedding ring; no, we do not have any specific rituals requiring their attention.

Yes, this policewoman has come in, but only halfway in, so the door is still open behind her, with the long hallway stretching off, and I'm looking past her like maybe my dad will step out from behind a closed door and take this bag himself. These are his things.

"We found his wallet some distance from the corner. He must have been holding it at the time of the accident."

Of course he was holding it. "And his lottery tickets?"

She frowns.

Because I see him. Returning from the store with his supper. On foot despite the weather, wearing his great navy overcoat, his rain hat, his scarf. I see the canvas bag over his shoulder with its two bottles of beer at the bottom, the Kit Kat bar, a freshly wrapped piece of fish. Those lonely goddamn carrots. Maybe a carton of eggs for his breakfast. And in his gloved hand, his three scratch tickets. He would have had his nickel out, his tickets gripped in his fingers. His wallet folded up but not yet back in his pocket. He would have waited for the crosswalk. I know this about my dad. Even if he didn't look up when he stepped out into the road.

The woman holds the bag out toward me again but she stops her hand this time and redirects it toward Neil. I can see it on her face, this idea that maybe he'll take it from her. The husband, the son-in-law, the one who appears to be calmer. But Neil just stares at the bag.

I turn to George—small, wiry George, my dad's best friend. His workman's hands are clenched and tense, held tight against his sides. How long has George been here? Of course, I remember with relief, because I need to keep things straight, George has been here longer than we have. He's the one who called us, called us for nearly an hour until he finally reached Neil. Needing to tell us to get to this hospital as quickly as we possibly could. His face is tired with the length of time he's been waiting, waiting here alone as we drove over the mountains to meet him. Beside us there are others talking—a doctor, a surgeon, a woman with glasses in a navy blue sweater—they're speaking so quietly, it's like everything is normal. So I snatch the bag of my dad's belongings, hurl it hard against the wall beside them and watch everyone duck as the bag splits and the items fly backward across the room. Nothing about this moment should be normal.

The surgeon crosses to me and takes my shoulders in a pair of strong hands. I give him my full attention and it quells the heat that is flooding through me. Here is a man with so many lines on his face. A man just about the same age as my dad. His voice is extremely calm and although I don't hear everything he says, I do catch something about "did not suffer" and "unconscious" and I know what he's doing, and so I nod and say "thank you". What I'm really hoping is that he might reach out and punch me right in the face.

Ashamed, I breathe hard, lean down to pick up everything I've thrown.

"I'll help you," says the woman with the perfectly nice blue sweater, kneeling down beside me.

"Don't touch them," I say. These are my dad's things and no one else should be able to touch them. She stills, crouched, watching me.

None of these items make any sense. Keys. A watch. I see the wallet she mentioned. His rubber coin purse and the cell phone I gave him for his birthday. The screen isn't even cracked. The Washington State Ferry pin from his coat. Credit cards and loyalty cards. Receipts. Yes, these are my dad's things.

I see him again. At the door of the house, fumbling in his pockets, hunting for his keys. He would have put them in his left jeans pocket. He would have checked for them twice as he walked down the street.

His yellow rain hat tight at the chin. Like he was just heading out to the boat. Like he had a fishing pole on his shoulder and not his shopping bag. Alone as usual. The woman stands up. I am grabbing items from the floor—a folded grocery list, another credit card. But alongside these items is a photostrip. The stark white border draws the eye. It's a rectangle of photo-cabin slides like the ones my dad and I used to take when I was younger. It seems perfectly natural that he would still have had one of these in his wallet. And that it would have gotten separated somehow, dislodged from alongside his money and driver's license and launched into the street with the force of the impact.

I'm looking carefully now, eyes narrowing, remembering years and years before when I would meet my dad at the ferry docks after school. Remembering how we liked to document the day with a series of photos from the instant photo box at the Pier. Black and white markers of our age progression: me at thirteen with braces and glasses, at fifteen with a long ponytail and my first pair of contact lenses, at sixteen when my dad shaved his beard for the first and only time.

I keep staring at these photos, trying to figure out when I have recently taken this kind of picture again. I look so old.

But I'm not that old. I reach for the photo, think to retrieve it from the floor and bring it closer to my eyes, but my hand doesn't reach its target. It isn't me in the photos.

This is how my mother reappears. Impossibly. Like a ghost ship washed up in a bright clean harbor.

"Wait, is that you?" Neil asks, reaching for it.

I am much faster than he is. I snatch the photostrip and am up and across the room into an empty chair, the half-refilled bag still in my hand. I curl my chest over these pictures, hold them to my belly and breathe and breathe and breathe until the desire to vomit passes. If I curl myself tight enough than this, too, won't be happening and maybe no one else will see what the ocean has cast up before us. Especially not Neil. Neil can't be allowed to see this. He knows nothing of the ocean and he cannot possibly understand.

Someone asks me what's wrong. The nurse and the woman in the blue sweater are conferring rapidly. George has cocked his head at me.

"Ella?" he says.

"How dare she," I say. Because I made the bargain the summer I turned ten, the summer of Lizzy, when I agreed to give up my mother if I could keep my dad. I have held up my end of things but like always she has backed out of the trade. Like always, she has ruined everything.

Neil crosses to me, kneels beside me. He smells of panic and of our closed up car and its journey across the snowy Cascades to get to my dad. So why can't someone bring him in here? Because he would know what to do, he knows all about the sea. I close my eyes and I see the two of us watching for boats, how we loved the sound of the waves, how he always knew exactly how to take us safely across the water. That's what I want.

I open them and see George, and I stand quickly because I could hand him the photos. Yes, he can take them. Nothing will have to be said and no explaining will have to be done. But my God, he looks so tired, his face gray and tight. I keep the photos flattened against me, until the policewoman begins to step backward through the door and I try to follow her, waving the bag at her, waving the photostrip. Maybe I can just hand all these items right back.

It's too late. The woman is gone and Neil is up and beside me craning his neck—gently, his curiosity is so innocent and gentle— to see these photos, to actually see her face. And who can really blame him?

"You look … I mean, it's so surprising. You're the same," Neil says.

I know what to do. I hold tight onto this strip of three black and white photos and I rip them. I rip and rip, separating the glossy paper along the white spaces. Then I make a stack of them in my hands and shuffle them over and over like maybe the woman who isn't me might go away if I keep placing her at the bottom of the stack.

"Ella?" George says. "What the hell is this?"

But it isn't a real question. There's no way to answer him. *This* is a photo of my mother inside my dad's wallet. *This* is also my dad's wallet inside a plastic bag. I want neither of these things.

The room is silent then. George. Neil. Me. The surgeon. Another doctor, or maybe this person is a nurse. The blue sweater woman is rubbing her left wrist with her right hand. But she stops and reaches for me, tries to put her hand on me too. It comes to me that she's the counselor. The person meant to manage all the emotions in the room. She says, "It's okay to be upset, Ella. What can we do right now to help you?"

So I say, "Why couldn't you have found her body in a dumpster instead?" I have always been able to handle this idea. This has always been part of the trade.

Everyone looks at me sharply. No one says a thing.

4

It's late May. School will be out in just over a week. I'm in line for the bus when I spot her and it startles me, but just at first. It's good she's up and about. I shoulder my back pack and walk over so she sees me too. When she does, her smile breaks wide and I know everything will be fine today. What I don't know is that this is the last summer. But neither does she, so right at this moment we're even.

She's wearing her hair tucked beneath a beaded head-scarf, she's tied a gold fabric around her waist that has a little bell, and she's wearing a long skirt. She jingles as she walks. She's come to meet me after school, something she hardly ever does anymore.

When she sees me walking her way, she holds up her hands and says, "Shall we dance?"

I smile, shake my head and fall in step beside her.

"Got everything?" she asks me. Then she stops, pulls a tissue from a pocket in her skirt and blows her nose, stuffing it back away when she's done. She announces, "Doctor says I'm just lucky I didn't get pneumonia. But what he doesn't know is how strong these lungs are."

And it's true. She's been sick for months but she never coughs. She keeps the cold in its place.

"Are you wearing a costume?"

"I found it in the attic, isn't it marvelous?"

"So what does it make you?"

"Huh?"

"What does it make you?" I repeat, a little louder. "A fortune teller?"

"I think it belonged to Grandma Sourmany." She twirls once, throws her head back and dances a funny cross-step. "I think she must have worn it for her wedding."

It doesn't matter that I can still remember a previous Halloween, of hunting for costumes with her at the Goodwill and of her wrapping me up in this same scarf amidst the aisles of men's coats. It does look like something Grandma Sourmany might have worn a long time ago. "It's beautiful," I tell her.

"You're just wearing this on the inside, you're just as beautiful."

She reaches down and takes my hand. Gives it a squeeze. I squeeze back. The late bus passes us then, and there's Alex White sticking his tongue out at me from the back window. If she wasn't with me, I'd flip him the bird.

The jingling quiets and her face stills. "What's that kid about?"

I try to squeeze her hand again but she pulls it away. "He's just stupid," I say, waiting for her face to smooth itself out again. "He doesn't matter."

"Is he in your class?"

I shake my head. It is really important she turn back at me. "You should be wearing some big hoop earrings with that, don't you think? We could go find some."

But her gaze stays fixed on the bus. Her hand flutters up to her mouth; she presses three fingers to her lips and her eyes narrow.

"Or big fake rings," I try again, my voice too high. "Like ten of them, like the movies. We could go to Luke's and hunt in the jewelry bins."

Nothing. She's staring and I'm thinking hard and fast about what I might do but then she drops her hand and shrugs. "I really don't think I need to worry too much about him, do you?"

No, I'm thinking, you don't have to worry about him. It's just stupid Alex White and we do not have to follow him or call his mom or do anything that will embarrass me. It takes her a minute, but she lets it go and my body relaxes as we fall into step.

We walk up the street and she's gliding along. Her leather sandals silent but her skirt and scarf tinkling with each step. Kids pass us on their bikes. We wave to neighbors. She stops to talk to old lady Stevens and when I keep going, she puts her hand on my shoulder and I know to stay put. Right beside her. Her hair touches my cheek when I stand that close; she's left it down but brushed it out and it's wild, electric, the tips frizzing. It's like her when she's being fun.

We say goodbye to Mrs. Stevens and my mother says we need to stop at the grocery store. "I had extra work," she tells me as we walk through the doors. "I didn't have time to get anything before getting you."

"Busy day?" I ask. My mother works part time at O'Sullivan's Flowers. She doesn't usually work on Wednesdays. "Did they need you special?"

She raises her eyebrows at me, then peers around the shop. There are a lot of people—older kids from the middle school mostly, but there are also a few young mothers with their strollers and some other adults. Classic rock is playing on the overhead speakers and my mother frowns as she cocks her ear to it, then starts mouthing along with the song.

She leans down and her voice is loud in my ear, "Get me a can of pineapple, El." Then she pulls a list from her pocket. "And the big container of Nancy's yogurt. Meet me back here."

But when I get to the yogurt section she's just behind me. "We need butter. I forgot." A woman in the aisle startles; my mother has practically shouted. I smile at the woman because I have learned that this helps.

I take the butter we always buy, put it in our basket. My mother is watching the other woman walk away.

"Mom?" I have to say this twice. Then, "What else, Mom?"

She checks her list, still bobbing her head to the music, and asks me to grab some mayonnaise from the second aisle. "I'll get wine."

But she stays with me instead.

"I can get it," I say, turning around to face her. "Mayonnaise and whatever else we need. Meet you at the check-out."

But she just says, "Ice cream for dessert?"

I nod. I don't offer a second time.

We get the ice cream and join the check-out line. We wait, not talking, and I shift to look at the magazines just beyond the cashier. She stops me, "Stay starboard, it's nearly our turn."

It isn't, but I don't argue.

This is when the elderly couple behind us lean forward, smiling at each other and at us. The woman giggles and raises her eyebrows, "I think I know a boating family when I hear one."

Out of the corner of my eye I am watching my mother. Gathering my clues for how I should respond. She doesn't smile at first, but then she does—slowly, widely.

The man squares his thin shoulders and says, "Chief Engineer. Oil tankers. Forty-seven years of service."

"My dad's a Chief Mate," I tell them quickly, checking my mother's face, but she doesn't seem to mind what I've said. "He'll be Captain soon."

He nods in approval. "Chief Mate's a big deal. Lucky girl! But how'd you like to spend four months in the engine room of one of the big boats? A captain can't do anything without a well-run engine room. Young lady, I've fixed more axles than you can imagine!"

We move forward in the line, and I'm glad because I don't have to say anything to that. I cannot imagine such a skinny old man would be strong enough to fix anything in the engine room of a ferry. I've watched Leonid on my dad's boat unwinch a broken cable in two seconds, his thick arms streaked with grease.

"You and your engine rooms," the woman says, rolling her eyes, and fiddling with the vegetables in her basket. "Always trying to get people into them. No one else likes all that noise."

"I love the engines," I say, proud of my knowledge of the boat.

My mother shushes me. "You've only seen one a few times." To the woman, she says, "And they are noisy."

"I'll take you to mine, little lady," the man says, winking at me. "You'll like it so much, you'll never want to get out. Every boat needs a good oiler, and my boat needs someone just about your size!"

The woman speaks to my mother in a lower voice, "Personally, I can't stand to go down in them. They're so dark."

My mother nods, but her smile is gone. Her hand on my shoulder has grown tight. We turn away because anyway it's now our turn.

After we've paid and are walking away, I hear the woman say, "Have a nice day," but my mother doesn't turn around. I turn and wave, but my mother takes me by the elbow and tells me to hurry along.

We are still crossing the parking lot, each of us carrying a plastic bag from the shop, when she asks me about school. She's walking fast now and her skirt jingles furiously with each step.

"It was great," I say. "Really great."

"You're still doing the continents in social studies?"

We finished them a month or so ago but I nod anyway. "Antarctica's my favorite. Penguins are funny."

"Penguin moms will sometimes kidnap another mom's chick."

Not wanting to be outdone, I say, "Wild penguins aren't afraid of humans," I say. "So people who go to see them can get really close. That isn't good, right?"

But she doesn't answer. She's stopped to watch a car drive past. In the front seat are the man and woman from the store. My mother is frozen, her eyes following the wood-paneled minivan. First, only her head swivels but then she turns completely around. The car is already a half-block away when she snaps her fingers and says, "Quick, do you have some paper?"

"Why?"

"Can I have some?" Her eyes are on the car. "Quick, El."

I slip my backpack from my shoulders, unzip it and reach inside. "How big?"

"I don't care. Small's okay."

"Here," I hand her a ripped half-page from my Social Studies notebook.

The car is three blocks away by now, but she whips a pencil out from inside the fold of gold fabric at her waist and writes something down. She hesitates a second, folds the paper, unfolds it, writes a few more words, and stares at it hard.

"What is that? What's wrong with those people in that car?"

She doesn't answer me.

"Mom?"

But she shakes her head. Then she tucks the pencil with the paper back into her waist, watching the car until it vanishes finally, turning left down a side street.

"Some people," she says, shaking her head and staring up the empty street. She doesn't finish the thought.

"They were nice," I say.

Her head swivels around. "What?" The irises of my mother's eyes are sharp. Her hand rises to her throat and her left cheek.

"I thought they were nice," I say. Try as I might, I cannot work out why my mother is so interested in them.

"Oh, nice," she says, dropping her hand and frowning at me. "Yes, that's the word."

5

SOMEONE HAS TO CARRY THE NEW BAG OF my dad's belongings out of the hospital and the three of us can't seem to decide who should do it. Neil is holding it as we leave the office, but I take it from him before we hit the lobby. I hold it tight but cannot keep my fingers still; I twist the thin plastic, wrap it tight around my thumb until the blood is cut off and my finger starts to throb. In the space between the two sets of sliding glass doors I pass it to George, who takes it with a confused look on his face. He passes it back to me, but I hand it right over again.

"What the hell, Ella?" he says. I want to reach toward him, smooth out his frown and the wrinkle in his forehead, but instead, I'm nodding like this is all perfectly natural. You should have this, George, I'm thinking, he's your best friend.

"Maybe you can fix the watch." I say.

Then George stops and we all stare at the cracked glass of my dad's watch. It's been cracked for a month or so, this has nothing to do with the accident. I think of how many times I told my dad over the last few weeks that he should just take it in to get it fixed.

"If you wait any longer the face is going to fall off," I hear myself telling him. "You'll have to get an entirely new watch."

"No time," he says, smiling at his own joke.

No, he does not say this. So I must put one foot in front of the other and leave the hospital. George has gone on ahead of us toward the cars, is standing in the middle of the parking lot with the bag in his hands. He's swiveling his head right and left and I know he's lost his car, I know, too, that he shouldn't be allowed to drive himself back home. But none of us are willing to come back here tomorrow to pick up a left-behind car. So I watch him disappear into a long row of dark vehicles and then Neil and I are standing next to our own car. We open the doors and Trapp greets us with fitful leaps and nose presses. He calms down quickly when we do not respond in kind.

We drive off in silence. Out of the parking lot, onto the freeway. Neil's hands on the steering wheel, my boots on the floor, my knees shaking, my hands fluttering around and over the pocket of my jacket with the torn photos. Why did he have these? Why? But I don't really want to know why, what I want to know is how will I make it all go away? And how will I keep Neil out of it? The rain against the window blurs the hard edges of the trucks and cars. Neil passes a minivan and then merges the car into the far right lane. The freeway is so busy— what could all these people have to do outside of their homes at this hour? In this rain? I watch it. I listen to it as Trapp fidgets and whines from the back seat. He tries to jump into my lap but I block him. We keep driving north. We cross over Lake Union and I don't turn my head to seek out the black line of water and mountains to the west.

And then, somewhere after the bridge, there beside us in the lane to the right in his own car, is George. He's staring straight ahead, both hands on the wheel; he doesn't see us and I don't try to get his attention. I think how strange it is that we are in separate cars but living the same event. I wonder where Lisa is—why didn't she come with him to the hospital? I want to think it's because she's working, but I know it probably has something to do with her daughter and her grandkids and the trouble there. Poor George, I think, but then I am thinking, poor me, and kicking the floor of the car, punching with my fist against the glove box. It falls open and its messy contents spill down onto the floor. I stomp them down and then down again, crush an empty paper cup, grind a few receipts and other paper debris into the wet carpet beneath my boots. Crows do this, I think. Crows gather in the hundreds around the body of a dead crow and in their rage and despair they may tear it to pieces trying to work out what has happened. And this is what I want—to split myself into a hundred little winged bodies and attack.

Neil reaches a gentle hand to my shoulder and so I must settle. I breathe. I do not settle, but in twenty years I have grown very good at making it seem that I have.

"This is just insane," Neil begins, his voice wavering. "Unbelievable, I mean. I just don't understand."

He continues, "I just don't believe it."

Then, "But those photos, El? What do they mean?"

Of course Neil is far too ready to accept this evening's exchange. This will seem easier for him.

"I had to Lethal the Knemeyer's dog this morning," I say, talking fast, saying the first thing that comes to my mind. We cannot talk about my mother. Not Neil.

His head turns at the change of subject, turns back to the road.

"I had to bite glove, and take her on." I rub one palm with the thumb of my other hand. "Can you believe I was strong enough?"

"What happened, what are you talking about?"

"They never should have bred her. I told you that. You remember I told you that?"

"Yes," he says, vaguely a question. His voice is patient. He thinks I'm not being coherent.

"She was deranged after whelping. It was horrible. She went after the puppies. And Nathaniel and Caitlin...I could have hit Nathaniel." And I mean this. I think about how it would have felt to take my anger out on my client. In the thought are the dog's eyes and the tilt, too. I shake my head.

Neil shifts his legs because we're driving in my car and he doesn't fit but he hasn't bothered to adjust the seat. He's all hunched over like he's been punched in the gut. I want to tell him to relax, to stretch his legs. I want to help him unroll from this punch.

But then he says again, "You didn't know he had those photos, did you? I thought she was ..." He doesn't finish his sentence because I've never given him the right word to do it easily. Dead? Missing?

I close my eyes. Tight as my fists. Create a darkness. "It's not really that," I say. "Something doesn't fit. The photos must be old." The photos are in my pocket. I don't reach for them. I open my eyes to a wall of blurry, glaring tail lights.

"Tell me again how long since he's seen her?"

"It's not like that, Neil."

"I don't know." He pauses. "There must be some kind of explanation. He's never said a thing? My Aunt Besta left a letter for her children. You know about that."

Because it's so easy for Neil to think of his family, his mercifully ordinary family whose greatest secret—which they laughingly tell everyone at dinner parties—involves an Old World relative who once left her children to sneak across an ocean and sing in a New York City nightclub. A family whose shared vocabulary does not include shameful terms like persecutory interpretations or maladaptive behavior.

We are at our exit. George's car is some lengths behind us. It will continue on one more exit and make its way home. Neil takes our car off the freeway and drives the few blocks to my dad's house. He avoids the intersection of the accident, but I see it anyway, see the bright lights of the supermarket with its Scandinavian flags, the new pharmacy, the sushi place. I see the wide lanes and the traffic. There is always so much traffic. I see the cars. I see my dad. Then I close it all down and I see nothing.

When we pull up to the house, I open my door to let Trapp jump out onto the lawn, stepping after him into the pouring rain. I watch Trapp sniff along the parking strip and zigzag around the small tree trunks. Neil is taking our bags from the car, holding his coat over his head, and I take two steps toward the side door but then I stop. I was here just a few weeks ago. Just a few weeks ago I walked up these front steps and into the living room and there was my dad watching a football game with George. I can still hear the televised cheering and my dad's shouts and fist-shaking at the screen. I see his long legs stretched before him, his beard, his hand wrapped around a can of beer. Even through the storm, I can hear him. I know exactly what he'd be saying.

From behind the side door come the yelps and whimpering of Daisie. How long has she been alone? Since he went out to get his groceries. Why didn't he take her with him? This change in the events of his evening would have made all the difference. I think of the time it might have taken for him to put Daisie on her leash, the way she would have slowed him down by sniffing at trees and greeting other walkers and dogs. All of this would have worked in my dad's favor. He would have been that many seconds later and maybe that pick-up would have passed through the intersection before he stepped into it, maybe that pick-up would have made a butterfly of someone else's ribcage—I close this thought down, how ugly it makes me to wish for this kind of trade.

Neil comes up beside me, his pale face crumpled with dark shadows. "Can you take this?"

Of course I cannot, I think, I cannot take this.

But he hands me a backpack and nods toward the back door.

We walk inside. Past the grateful whimpers of Daisie who cannot decide whether to sniff us, growl at Trapp, or pee on the floor. Past the last dishes my dad used, washed and dried and standing at mournful attention on the sideboard next to a neatly folded dishtowel, and on into the living room. I stop near the dining room table, find that my body has made a complete halt. My legs will not move. My hands will not move. The trunk of my body is fixed to the hardwood floor of this room. The backpack I'm carrying slides to my feet. Daisie is back inside from her race around the yard, is now circling my legs, asking for love. But still I cannot move. Trapp is nudging me from behind, pressing his shoulders into the backs of my knees. Still I stand steady. But Neil turns, understands. Knows to come back for me. He helps me through the living room and up the stairs into my old bedroom, long since converted to a guestroom. I sit on the bed until I can hold it no longer and then I throw up in the wastepaper basket next to a photograph my dad took of his Bleeding Heart shrub, the summer before, in full glorious bloom.

6

A SHIP'S USEFULNESS IS NOT IN ITS SIZE or the number of decks it is lucky enough to have. "Sure," my dad used to say, "The Titanic had ten decks, but that didn't help matters, did it?"

I always agreed. I knew what he meant. Every boat had a purpose and that was all that mattered. Cargo or fishing or ferrying. Leisure or work.

"And they can change, don't forget."

"Sure, they can."

We spoke in code, our own code, but we always knew what we were saying to each other.

"Because there isn't anything wrong with scaling back," he would say.

"Aye, aye, Captain," I'd answer.

"The thing of it," he said once, "is that sometimes you have to razee what you originally had, remove the upper deck and re-purpose the vessel."

I knew about the HMS *America*, the *Independent*, about the French warships, the British sloops, the American gun-whalers. I knew my dad's stories because this is how we beat George on trivia nights, how we made bets with the other Captains and the crew on long Saturday runs up to the peninsula and weekend fishing trips with friends from work and the neighborhood.

"Tell 'em, El," my dad would say,

And I'd tell them how the wood of a top deck gets shaved right down, how they melt the pig iron and re-mount the fittings, how they cut new port windows and save the best of the wood for the doors. I'd tell them how the HMS *America* was cut down from a third rate to a fourth rate and used during the Oregon boundary dispute, that what mattered was the number of gun decks and maneuverability in Pacific coastal waters and so sometimes you just had to make something smaller, lighter. The HMS *America* had fewer crew members, stronger guns. The mates loved it when I talked like that.

"Son of a sailor, Ella Tomlinson, don't you just know your stuff."

Yes, I would think. Smaller. Less decks. Increased stability. That way we could move as fast as we needed to. We could choose our harbor. Forget about her.

7

I MANAGE A FEW HOURS OF SLEEP BUT THEN I wake before dawn with another roll of nausea. This time I don't throw up, I lie perfectly still and wait for my stomach to unknot itself. Neil gets up, goes downstairs, and then comes back with two mugs of tea and asks me how I'm doing as he hands me mine. I don't answer, because what is there to say? As my mind rose from sleep into the dark of the guestroom, for a fraction of a second I didn't know where I was and for that fraction of a second, I had forgotten what has happened.

But then I knew. Now I know again.

I wrap my fingers around the mug, hold tight to the scalding ceramic.

We are here in my dad's house and my dad is not here with us. And somewhere downstairs my coat is draped across the back of a chair. In its pockets is the trade that must be someone else's idea of a very bad joke: my dad for my mother.

Yet this is exactly what I have suggested to clients over the years when one of their animals has died and left behind a grieving mate or friend. Just a few months ago I gave the idea to a local farmer when her pony stallion passed away and her mare refused to eat and began spending all its time alone in the corner of the paddock or standing on the spot where the stallion had fallen the day he died. I told her to put the mare in a smaller paddock with a new pony, or a dog, or even a goat. She did as I suggested and within a few short weeks the sad little pony had bonded with a sheepdog puppy, was eating again, had seemingly forgotten her loss.

This would suggest that love is nothing but habit. And don't people say it only takes three days to get out of one. I can't even remember what day it is today, let alone count forward three days and imagine that I might accept my mother like she were nothing but an affectionate sheepdog pup and I were a stupid, forgetful old pony.

Neil slides back into bed, rests his head behind him on the headboard. Drinks his tea. I take a few more sips from my mug. Feel the burn of the liquid on my tongue, on my throat. We have not turned on the bedside light and I have no idea what time it is; outside it is still very dark.

We whisper to each other across the bed. We say things like, "we should take showers," and "are you hungry?" and "I hope George made it home okay." We are polite and careful. I worry he left the headlights on, but he says he double-checked. I worry we left our house in Wenatchee unlocked, but he tells me that he locked it. I worry about the Wolfhound and the tabbies, about the rabbits and the hamster, about the message the clinic has left me about a cat that ingested several pills its owner had accidentally dropped on the floor. I worry that it won't make it because its liver was so damaged.

"What if this cat dies in the night?" I say.

"It will be alright."

"It might not."

"It might not, but it probably will."

"How can you be so sure?"

There is a long pause. A deep breath.

"I'm not sure, I'm only hopeful."

My long pause. My deep breath.

"Do you have enough to share?"

And then we are putting our mugs on the floor and meeting in the middle of the bed in a commotion of hands and limbs and mouths. At first Neil's hands on me are like an erasure; each soft movement of palm and finger against thigh against breast against throat against hip and I lose a few seconds of myself. Here is a trade that does not feel like a cheat. My eyes close, my ears fill with the sound of the sheets, of our skin, of our breathing. Neil covers and contains me and I can stretch this quiet act to make it a new frame. Today's frame. I breathe and move and give.

But then it stops working. The intensity we would usually move toward shifts further and further away until I'm like a swimmer who's lost her breath and I just want to get up and out of the water but Neil is holding me under. I'm pulling on his shoulders and pushing him away at the same time. My body angry and closed down. I need air. I need space. He stops. We wait. I hear him shudder and he could be crying, or maybe he's made his way to his own solitary climax.

It may be minutes later or hours later, but I become aware again of how chilly the room has grown, how crisp and rough the sheets feel against my legs and arms. Neil is a weight to my left, but I cannot detect his body heat. Has he been sleeping? Have I been sleeping? I cannot perceive a change in the darkness outside.

His voice is quiet, seems to come from a fixed distance. "Are you okay?"

"I'm keeping my carry-on stored safely under the seat."

His head rustles its agreement against the pillow and I sit up, wracked again by yet another wave of nausea. I breathe through its highest point until it breaks and settles but the last forty-eight hours compress and I think hard.

"Got your own footprints, Ella?" Caroline teased me the day before yesterday when I turned down her famous carrot cake because the smell made me gag. Footprints. What I tell farmers and other clients when an insemination of one of their animals has been a success because the ultrasound of the early embryo, no matter the species, often has the shape and form of the sole of a shoe. I waved her away, apologizing, speculating a stomach bug. The bug, of course, has not materialized and I count backward now as if this might help. I try to remember my last period, but can't because sometimes my periods don't come for months, then they come for weeks at a time. I tap a fingertip to my belly and I think, no, it can't be that. There's really no chance because it couldn't have worked. It shouldn't have.

I open my mouth to say something to Neil but I close it again. I jump out of bed and race down the stairs. Shivering, shaking with cold. The dogs leap up from their beds in the office and race after me. Trapp nips at my heels. I shoo them away. Find my coat. Take out the photos. I stand in the living room and I look at the photos, all three of them. My mother. My mother. My mother. I have to hold one hand with the other to stop my trembling. She is not smiling. Or maybe she is. A small curve to her mouth. Her hair is still very dark red but streaked with gray. Neil calls to me from upstairs but I ignore him, go into the downstairs bathroom and lock the door. I do not turn on the light, leaving myself in the blue of the streetlamp light that angles in from the outside window. I drop the photos on the floor but I can see the same thing in the mirror. My hair the same dark red. Long like hers. Our mouths unsmiling. Our eyes open, staring. I'm still shivering hard so I pull open the glass shower door and turn on the hot water. Neil is calling from outside the door and I call back that I'm freezing, that I need to warm up. My voice sounds normal to me. How on earth have I managed this? I still haven't turned the light on and I step on one of those photos as I reach for a towel in the closet. I step on her face.

The shower is far too hot but I don't adjust it, I just stand there under the water. My skin burns, my feet start to prickle, but still I don't move. The spray from the shower hits me full on the neck and I concentrate on the pain, tilting already, wondering if I make it any hotter would I get an actual burn?

"Ella, you must see this," she whispered, and I see her again, pointing at a person on a boat two slips over from ours at the marina. The man's skin is pink and brown, stretched too-tight over the nose, wrinkled around the lips and eyes. "He's been burned," she continues, still keeping her voice low. "Someone burned him." Really? Did someone burn him? Why would someone do that? What if it was just an accident? But no, she is adamant. She is always so sure of what she says. "Someone must have burned him. Someone must have been really angry."

It's so hot in this shower, the steam is choking me and I have to sit down at the far end of the tub because I'm going to throw up again. I retch and I retch but nothing comes up. There is nothing for my body to let go of.

I rinse my mouth anyway, rinse myself one last time and get out. The room is immediately cold again and my towel is an old one, patchy in places, the trim frayed at the bottom, a relic left over from my childhood. It doesn't do its job so I must rub and rub to dry every single inch of my body. I stand wrapped in the towel in the middle of the room and I close my eyes. I wait. I wait. I wait. It starts to work.

It isn't even difficult. There comes to me from somewhere across the house the sound of my dad's footstep, of his voice. I hear each footfall on the hardwood, coming closer. I hear the half-clearing of his throat, the way he always hesitates before raising his voice to call out. I know that I could open the door and he might be standing right there, ready to ask me what I'd like for breakfast. All I need to do is reach for the doorknob and open the door and everything will be just fine.

Keep level with those pylons, Captain.

Nah, we're in the clear. Sail on.

But then I'm shaking with another thought. How easy this was, how easily I have conjured him up.

"She makes things up," he told me once. "She's always done that. She makes things up about people and what they're doing. It's like a game. Your mom has the wildest imagination."

I remember asking him if she was wrong sometimes. I remember how quiet he grew, how he put a hand to my head, smoothing back my hair. His hand is so warm; he's been out on the boat all day. His face is glowing from the sun and the wind. In my memory we don't speak for a long time and the temperature of our skin where it touches—his hand, my forehead—slowly becomes exactly the same.

I know how to furl the sails, Captain. I pull on my jeans and my shirt, then I reach for the photos. Stare hard. They must be old photos, I think, stashing them in the bathroom drawer. They have to be. *Aren't they, Captain?* I finish getting dressed, taking deep breaths and panting out my lingering nausea like a dog. Then I do what I have been trained to do—I evaluate the state of the animal in my presence. I reduce myself down to my heart beat and my blood pressure and my fluid levels. Do I feel better? Maybe I should cry? Would it help? But my face won't seem to scrunch up, everything stays contained. I put two fingers to my wrist, try to follow those tiny little beats, I take deep breaths. But I can't seem to concentrate on the idea of what makes something better or what makes something worse; my mind just slips away to another kind of cataloging—the rasp at the back of my throat, the dripping of wet hair down my back, the ache around my jaw. And I think that this particular animal needs someone else's attention, someone who will know what to do.

I leave the bathroom to the sound of a chair scraping in the kitchen. I go to find Neil, arranging my face along the way. I can tell he's been waiting for me, the way he's sitting, the slope of his shoulders. He turns as I walk in and I can see the words that will come, the questions. I know how understanding he will be at first, but then one day when he sees it all more clearly, when he sees what might happen, he won't be understanding anymore.

"We need to make a list," I say before he can start, running a hand along his shoulder and sitting beside him. His mouth closes, and I take his fingers in mine and look into his eyes for a long minute. "How are you doing?"

He's staring at me, his mouth inverted in a frown. He looks terrible—unkempt, blotchy skin. He's been crying. Then I see what he's got in his hands. It's a piece of petrified wood.

"I found it for you," he says. "Yesterday."

He places it in the palm of my one hand. It's a beautiful piece. A solid chunk, all rust-colored and sharp-edged. Opal glints in the thin round cross-cut.

"Where'd you find it?"

"Up Swakane, with the class. It was just lying there, in a creek bed with some wash-out gravel."

This is his way. On our first date he handed me a barred owl feather with a split quill. Several times a week, he hands me things as he walks in the door: a frozen crocus, a piece of snakeskin colored a vivid green from mineral deposits, a rock covered in fish scales—he has a knack for finding exceptional objects while at work.

While I admire the petrified wood, I can see it building up inside him again. The need to talk, to go over the evening, to ask me what's going on. He runs a hand through his hair, eyes darting around the kitchen, from sink to window to the back door. His hand muscles tighten in my hand. His arm trembles.

"I'll make us breakfast," I say.

"It's all so awful," he says, ignoring what I've said, spilling over. "I had my mom on the phone, and I had to tell her. And she was asking how you're doing."

I nod at this. Neil's lovely family and their comfortable emotions. If they lived closer they would swoop in and take care of us, of him.

"And then my dad came on, and there was this moment that I didn't know what to say."

"Of course you didn't," I say.

His voice breaks, "Ella, how can you stand it?"

I shake my head because I can't stand it. All I can do is hold his hand with one of mine and clench the piece of petrified wood with the other, letting its spiky edges dig into the soft flesh of my palm.

"And we need to go through his stuff, and figure out what's what. About your mom." He pauses then, looks at me, looks down, looks back up, and I know what's coming. He can't help being curious. This past of mine I've been unwilling to share. "Clearly they've been in contact. Maybe we need to get a hold of her."

"I know, Neil. Okay, yes, I know, we do need to figure out what's what," I say. "There's so much to think about. Yes. And we need to figure out what to do with the dogs. Do you think Daisie will have any trouble? Sometimes she doesn't get along with Trapp. Should we consider asking George about Daisie?"

He blinks. "No. We'll take Daisie. Of course. But, El?"

"I know what you mean. I want to, I do. I just think we have to be smart about it. Trapp is trained for the clinic. Daisie isn't."

Neil is nodding slowly, I've shifted his attention an inch. Just enough. He's watching the dogs now. Remembering the times when Daisie growled at Trapp or vice versa. "We don't have to decide right now."

The dogs become aware of our focus on them, and then they're both nosing my leg, whimpering and twisting for attention, and whether it's because they're hungry or they have to go outside, I don't care, it's a chance to get out, get away. I wrap my arms around Neil's neck and hug him tight, say I'll just run them around the block, that the fresh air will do me good. I grab the dogs' leashes and whistle softly, calling them to follow me and then I'm stepping out onto the sidewalk in the dim dawn light. What will this light feel like? Surely not like any other day.

8

THE STREETS ARE EMPTY AND I RACE THROUGH them to the nearby pharmacy, leave the dogs outside and in less than five minutes I have what I need, and in less than three more I am in the public toilets at the neighborhood lake. The light is green, the room is cold and smells of stale urine, but all I care about is ripping open the box of the pregnancy test. I pull out the plastic tester, I stand over the toilet and I pee so hard on the stick that I splash my fingers and the bowl. There's nowhere to set it and I have to wipe my hands on my jeans, trying not to drop it and trying not to get pee everywhere.

I wait, holding the tester away from my face, counting out the seconds and thinking how ridiculous this is. How awful. I'm in a public toilet with a pregnancy test, my kind and gentle husband in a warm house a few blocks away, ignorant of who I really am, and all I can hope is that the second line won't appear and I can just forget about this mess. This was not supposed to happen. I am a woman with irregular periods, with uterine fibroids. We discussed this. That it might take years, that it might not work at all. The thought rises up—dark and secret—that I only agreed to try because I assumed it would never work. A second thought rises up, what an idiot I have been, forgetting the most important rule of the ocean: never turn your back on the waves. I thought I was safe. When I look down at the test and see that it's positive, I throw it into the garbage and slam the door behind me, choking on the icy dawn air.

The lake looms black and still at the end of the path, itself shadowed by the bony fingers of the winter-dead oaks and maples and the drooping branches of the fir trees. Close to the water, I let the dogs off the lead and watch them race forward. I wish I could get my body moving like that, fast and low to the ground, taken up with the smells of the earth and the feel of only the rocks and leaves beneath me. None of this was supposed to happen.

When I reach the lake and see George sitting on the bench, it isn't really a surprise. I've even maybe come here to find him. He and my dad met at this lake after dinner or on the weekends, near the small pier to fish, or to just sit on a bench and talk. He's wearing his fishing waders and is wrapped in a blanket instead of a coat. In one hand he's holding a cigarette while the other rubs the top of his hairless head like the answer to everything that's happened could be read like Braille beneath the skin of his skull.

He sees the dogs first, turning fast at the sight of Daisie. The disappointment on his face is brief, then he waves me over. He sucks hard on his cigarette.

"I thought you quit," I say.

"Fuck I care about cancer right now."

The dogs hover nearby, hunting insects in the brittle light. Behind us the stiff branches of a monkey tail tree support the thin limbs of a weeping willow that has overgrown its allotted space. George drops his hand from his head, adjusts his glasses and gives me a tired smile.

"Well, then," he begins, as if we have planned to meet up this way, as if we have something important to discuss.

Trapp flies at a group of clustered swans, chasing them into the lake. The shock of their flapping white feathers beats against the air around us. I don't have the energy to reprimand him, and he races farther along, riling them over and over again. Daisie is busy sniffing George's waders.

"How you holding up?" he asks, which I know means, I am not holding up, and I think the expression apt, as though our shock might be lodged deep inside our spines.

I say nothing, and George leans his head backward, stretches his arms across the back of the bench and closes his eyes. He doesn't move for so long that I think he might actually fall asleep like that. His breathing deepens and I look out across the lake. None of this was supposed to happen. The only thing visible is the murky shape of a rowboat, anchored off shore about eighty yards. I imagine the boat has no bottom, that it isn't simply sliced out of view by the water but that it's really just a floating shell and I think, nothing to it, I'm just seasick. That's all this is. I can be tough, make it all go away.

George's head snaps up. His voice is brisk. "Well, I didn't think I'd feel this angry."

I think about Neil. How he held me so gently while we tried to make love, thinking I would need to cry. But what I most wanted to do was bite into the flesh at his shoulder. Tear a piece away with my teeth if I had to.

I grip the bench near my knees. "A client told me once that anger's optimistic," I say, thinking, what utter bullshit, what crap.

George looks at me through a squint as he smokes his cigarette down to the filter, throws the butt into the lake and lights another one. I scoot away from him because I've never seen him throw anything into a lake except a fish he won't keep. And I'm right because he's jumping up then, throwing back his blanket and flinging his half-smoked cigarette onto the ground. His arms jerk with frustration. "I didn't even get to see him. Why is that so goddamn important?"

Neither of us got to see him at the hospital. This seems like a perfectly reasonable thing to be angry about.

He stomps around the bench working out his nervous energy. He reminds me of the older farmers I know in Wenatchee. Their gruff pride. Their unwillingness to admit how sad they are when a dog dies in their arms.

He throws his hands up to his face. "I saw him nearly every day of my goddamn life."

"You did," I say.

"It isn't fair," he says.

"You're right," I say. "It isn't."

"And now your mother of all things."

I turn away. "Anyway, Neil and I will make a list of everyone to call."

He takes in a breath, his energy spent. "The Ferry Service already knows. From the hospital. Something about policy for state employees. When I identified him, they said they would have to do this."

"Wait—what?"

He shakes his head. "It was a photo, El. A photo on a clipboard. I don't know, they took it in the ambulance. Before I got there, before you got there. Said they would need it if you had to make resuscitation decisions before you could see him."

We are silent. No one had a chance to make any decisions.

I remember now that the woman in the blue sweater told me this and about George identifying the patient when he was still a patient and not a body. That she thanked George for doing this job, that I said thank you, too, although why I would say this makes no sense to me anymore. Then the woman suggested we wait to see his body at the funeral home. When it would be easier. Why didn't I ask her what that meant? Why easier?

Trapp comes alongside me and I rub the scruff of his neck, letting him lean into me. I turn to George, make up something to say, "Do you want to help with the memorial service?"

"Yeah," he says, rubbing his head again, and then, "Thanks," and then a swift intake of his breath. "Goddammit all to hell."

The light has changed while we've been talking. My dad's ferry will be captained by someone else today.

George turns to me. A small vein pulses in the skin beneath one of his eyes. "I think we should contact your mother." When I say nothing, he continues, "Now there's a sentence I hadn't expected to ever say."

I stand up and walk to the water's edge. The little rowboat out on the lake has drifted closer to us. I turn to see if George can see it too, but he's got his hands over his eyes. We are both trying to block the sun striking the water. I focus my eyes on the line of trees just behind the park benches, and I clasp my hands together until the rising wave of fear in my belly crashes and disappears with the pain that blooms between the knuckles of my right hand. I want to walk over to those trees and hide myself among the branches.

Some of her best stories were about the trees and I see her standing by the biggest cedar tree in the back yard. I'm maybe six or seven and so this is when her pronouncements were still mostly silly. "This is the one," she shouts to me. "See," she says. "It's taller than the others. This is the one they used."

As the story goes, there were once pirates in Ballard. And buried treasure everywhere on the bluff over the water. "Easier to hide, easier to keep safe," she would say. Her eyes are sparkling, her hands twitching with an imaginary shovel. "It's too bad we can't dig for it."

"Why not?"

"We'd have to kill the tree. The gold coins are twined up in the roots now. But every once in a while a ruby or an emerald grows up the trunk and appears on a branch."

I don't believe her. I'm sure this can't be true.

"Ask the woman who lives in Beecher House. How do you think she paid for that place?"

Beecher House is my favorite of our whole neighborhood, with its big porch and dormer windows facing the sea. It's old and gabled and I just know there is a telescope on the top floor with its star-gazing deck. I just know it.

George has crossed his arms over his chest, is trying to stare down the sun. I know this face of his. A stubbornness that will set up and dig deep, that will ruin him for months as he works his way back to his natural cheerfulness.

When I walk back to the bench, I say, "How's Lisa?"

"Guess."

"I'm sorry."

He shrugs. "She wanted to be at the hospital, but …"

"I'm sure she did. It's okay. Tell her that it's okay."

George's girlfriend Lisa must drop everything from time to time to take care of her grandchildren. There is no question that this is what she must do. All of us in George's life have accepted this and so I do not say any of the things that all of us have been saying to him for years, about how good and patient he is, about how much Lisa loves him, about how we support him, about hoping that Lisa's daughter will figure things out, leave her violent husband, save the kids. I think these things, I send them to him with a nod and my hand on his sleeve. He lowers his head, and I think how only one thing in our lives has changed in the last twelve hours. Everything else goes on—jobs and spouses and pets and homes and friends. None of this has changed. And so even a very tall man can be just one small thing that will mean something to only a small circle of people. I stuff my hands between my knees, clench and unclench them, because I can't decide whether this is a relief or a tragedy.

He pulls something from his pocket with his other hand and the light catches on it between his fingers. It takes me a moment to recognize that it's a fishing lure. A yellow rooster tail with a dented silver plate. He twirls it between his thumb and first finger, letting it spin, letting the hook catch into the thick skin near his fingernails and then flipping it over. And this is how I know we are sitting where I learned how to cast as a child. Sitting in the spot where George and my dad have always done their fishing.

George curls into himself and coughs, although he may be covering a sob. "I missed our poker night on Tuesday. Haven't seen him since last week, damn it."

I nod. Yes, I think. Since last week. That is what it will all boil down to. Every day will be a kind of counting game. I saw my dad two weekends ago. I spoke to him this morning. The thin dawn light makes me squint and I must remind myself, no, you spoke to him yesterday morning.

He said, "Smooth as steel."

And he said, "Sadly, only two."

And he said, "But maybe it won't be as bad as you think."

He did not say, not once, not ever, "I am carrying recent photographs of your mother in my wallet."

Neil's face at the hospital rises up before me. His hand stretching for those photos. Such natural curiosity about the things I have not told him. The things I need him to know already, and to know to never mention in my presence. Better yet, to have forgotten. Here is the story and here is why it matters, but here is why we are never going to speak of it. Because this is what I've done. The me that Neil knows—the woman he met six years ago, the woman he married two years ago—that woman has worked very hard to forget these things. The me that Neil knows has nothing to do with those photos.

Except now there are these footprints, and I wonder where the embryo might be attached to the wall of my uterus, whether its microscopic vertebrae might already be visible on an ultrasound. I've seen so many ultrasound images of my uterus over the years—the normally smooth gray tissue dotted with those darker plum-shaped rounds. Growths that would prevent the implantation of any fertilized egg. I wasn't supposed to be able to get pregnant. Thought I would never have to explain anything, that it would all work out without ever having to bring her up.

"Don't forget the cabin," George says at the same moment I turn into his shoulder and whisper, "I'm pregnant, George."

But George hasn't heard me. Maybe I only mouthed the words. I leave his shoulder and lean back into the bench.

"The cabin," I repeat. I double check the bench and the street lamp, I check for rising water in the lake, I check for a sudden wind coming toward us from the highway. I check for some sign of the end of the world. This place is no longer familiar. Maybe this isn't where I learned how to fish. I remember a boat house. Maybe a whole line of benches.

"You won't want to sell it, will you?" George asks. And he sounds so worried that I must immediately reply, "No, no," I say, "I won't want to sell it."

And then I'm already laughing, choking on the absurdity of it. A cabin! Why would I want to sell a cabin!?! Little bites of pain cut at my ribs as the sound makes its way out of my throat. George draws himself up.

"Ella?"

I close my eyes, my laughter quieting as I hold my breath.

"You know I've always considered you my niece, considered your dad a kind of brother. He was the closest thing … to a brother for me."

Yes, yes, I know, George, I want to say, shocked to hear him working through these words. It should go without saying how much George is already my family. So instead, I say, spitting the words a little, "Well, you know, George, he was the closest thing to a dad for me."

His eyes fix on my face. I count four fine lines threading their way to the left of his right eye, up toward his bald temples. A vein twitches. His lip twitches. And then we're both laughing. Laughing like idiots. Holding our mouths and our bellies. It isn't even a real joke but it works and we keep laughing. Laughing until our stomachs cramp up. The noise gets the dogs interested in us again and they rub their faces against our knees and wag their tails. The swans glide closer then, softly along the surface of the black water like a fleet of miniature white ferries.

Which is when I lean into George and admit I don't know anything about my dad having a cabin.

9

AFTER, WE TOOK OUR TURNS AT THE HELM. Like all good sailors, we knew when to keep our mouths closed and when to just drive forward into the waves.

After, there were good parts and bad parts. One of the best parts was the sharp wind as the ferry veered north past Port Blakely, or catching a bucket of smelt at Agate Point and salt-grilling them on skewers on the beach. Barefoot and sandy in our sailing clothes. Sometimes the best part was staying up late on the ferry, doing my homework in the wheelhouse. Other times it was fried egg breakfasts and coffee before walking the dog.

Once it was getting lost in a foggy inlet in the old boat, miles from any real harbor. "Light us," my dad said, and I manned the chest-sized safety lamp and kept us clear from rocks and tree trunks. "Nothing can drown us," he said when we made it in, shivering but safe.

The bad parts got fewer and farther between. Having to tell a teacher I didn't need to make a Mother's Day card. Watching my dad shake his head when someone said, "And Ella's mom?" Buying Kotex for the first time, rolls of tissue stuffed into my underpants until I could get home.

The worst part was when she reappeared suddenly. Not for real, but the few times that tangible proof of her entered the house. A letter in the mailbox. Addressed to us, signed by a woman that seemed to be her, that wanted us to remember who she was but couldn't, for her part, remember why that might be so. My dad would check the post mark and drive if he could get there, or telephone if he couldn't. But he always returned without her, hung up without news of her. We confirmed with each other that she was gone. Before was an island, After an entire ocean.

So he taught me about navigating, about the danger bearing, and how to keep the boat from ever running aground. I knew we were fine.

"The first thing you need to do is find a same-side object," he said.

"Like a light?"

"Can be a lighthouse if you're lucky, can be a well-marked outcropping or a house on a bluff. But you find one on the same side as the danger spot and lay a line out to your current position, marking your magnetic bearing."

"Got it."

"But the most important part of a danger bearing is your prefix."

"NLT?"

His proud eyes made me taller.

"Not Less Than is starboard, Not More Than is port."

So we were charted correctly. That's how it worked. We kept our eyes on the point of danger, and we took bearings as often as we needed—we kept away from it. We continued on. We kept the past in the past.

10

EARLY SUMMER. GEORGE BLOWS SMOKE out of his nostrils and leans over the tide pool. "Would you look at that?"

The pool is narrow but deep, rimmed with barnacles and sea squirters. A dark green anemone waves its spikes as the water slops with a wave below. Then a ripple disturbs the surface. A flash of red and white fins.

It's a curious fish, smaller than George's hand and reddish brown with white patches like clouds. It has wing-like fins and its face is flat, with the thick downturned lips of a bottom feeder. I lean down, waiting for George to tell me what it is and relieved to have this discovery between us. A distraction.

I watch him finish his cigarette, watch how he kneels and dips the tip in a small scoop of wet rock to extinguish it completely and then he tucks it into his pocket.

Only then does he say, "Sculpin. It's a Snubnose Sculpin." To the fish, he says, "A bit far north, aren't you, little one?"

I stare into the dark water, stop myself from reaching out to press the squirters, and wait for the fish to re-surface. I am with George today because my mother is missing. Or she was. I mean, she was missing but now she's coming back tomorrow. So right now, while I'm with George, she is in between missing and not missing. And this is the third time I've had to stay with George since school let out, because my mother has gone missing and come back already two other times.

The Sculpin's dorsal fin swishes above the surface then dips again below. I say, "It's stuck in here. Unless the tide comes in soon." I want to stay and watch the ocean rush in and carry the fish back into the waves.

"It'll die, though, if there's no outlet and the pool dries up before the next tide comes in."

My voice cracks. "But this pool is deep."

"It's not that deep."

I duck my head because fishermen are not crybabies. I see the fish's carcass bleaching white against the gray rocks like a vein of quartz, its gills venting open and closed as it gasps for air.

"That's how it goes, Elly," George says. His voice is gentle. "Life of the ocean."

I wipe hastily at my face because I understand what he's really saying. The fish needs my help, needs someone to take care of it. I stretch out flat on my belly to get a closer look; the fish swims toward me, surges upward so its dorsal fin arches above the water and then slips back under.

George hoots, maybe with a bit too much force. "I don't believe it. Now it's just showing off."

We watch the Sculpin slide along the rocks, and then George sighs, "Beautiful thing, isn't it? Now, watch it change colors as it hits that seaweed." And it does, slowly from red to brownish orange and then to a kind of green.

"How does it do that?" I ask.

"Sculpins'll change like a chameleon. We used to call them water lizards."

But the bigger question is what to do now that I've decided to help her. Of course Lizzy is a girl.

"You think we could try and get her in the catch bucket?"

George has already lit another cigarette and he takes a long drag, squinting his eyes. He blows the smoke over the top of my head. Then he nods, his lips pressed together. He helps me scoop Lizzy out of the tide pool. She swims into the plastic pail easily.

"We can let it go off the end of the jetty, so it's in deep water."

But I hold the bucket to the side, try to keep my voice clear. "I'm not going to let her go." The late afternoon sun hits me full in the face and I can't see George anymore.

His voice is worried. "Salt water fish are tricky."

"I know," I say, blinking hard. "I know. I can do the tank right. Anyway, I have a science project this summer."

He steps to the side and blocks out the sun. His face appears then, lined and serious. But he doesn't argue. He only nods toward our fishing rods and we head off the rocks and back to the jetty. We sit down together at the edge of the pier while George reaches into his pocket for his next cigarette. I pick up my fishing pole and he reaches to check the lure. He asks, "What kind of project?"

I've read how the downtown aquarium keeps their salt tanks, and I know I can make one, too. I figure I can re-create Lizzy's habitat, like I've learned.

"Study project," I say. "Scientific observations of rock fish."

"Sure," he says, shrugging. "Ok."

Maybe I can even find a male Sculpin, set them up as a pair. Surely none of the other kids will try something so difficult, and surely it will win me the science contest in September. But the biggest deal about this moment is that my mother is with me in this decision. *Scientific observations of rock fish* is something she would say if she were there and acting like herself. I can hear her. But she isn't there, she's missing, and although it isn't the first time and so far each time she's come back, she's also come back behaving less and less like my mother. I hold onto my fishing rod and sit with Lizzy in the small cooler beside me, and I feel what it would be like to have my mother right there, too. The feeling is so strong I think I could close my eyes and open them up to see her sitting on the next rock over, hair piled up on top of her head, legs stretched out in the sun.

"Fish aren't really animals," she might say. "They're more like dinosaurs. Their brains are so much older."

George speaks through the closed lips holding his cigarette, "Your mom tell you she was heading out somewhere this time?"

"Nah," I say, shaking my head, pretending it isn't a big deal.

"Did she call while she was away?"

"No, well, I don't know, but she went to Skagway."

"Skagway?!"

"That's what Dad said. I guess she wanted to try an Alaska boat." What he said was that she was checking out another ferry service. All the way up through Canada and into Alaska. And when I asked him why she'd want to do that, he said for "research" and then shrugged, like this explained everything. "You know how she is," he said. "How she gets focused on something. But she's on her way home."

It took her three days to get up there, but she's coming back tomorrow. I don't tell George that I have no idea how my dad finally figured this out. I don't tell George about sitting at the top of the stairs for two nights in a row, my stomach a hard, cold knot, listening to my dad call everyone we know and ask whether they've heard from her. Listening to him finally call the police.

"That mom of yours," George says. It's something he always said when she did something outrageous or funny. It's something he said all the time. And I knew what it meant.

Except today he says it in a whisper, and there's a dark shape behind the words.

"I know," I say, whispering back. "I know." Even if I don't know anything at all.

The next day is hot and sticky. George opens all the windows and all the doors of his small house. A family down the street is having a garage sale, and after a pancake breakfast at Denny's, we buy two wooden chairs and fall deep into the task of sanding and painting them. We are both acting like we aren't waiting for my parents to come back. Tom Petty blares from a boom box in the kitchen window. I have a paintbrush in my hand and I'm concentrating on not getting any drips on the grass when a horn sounds from the front. We both look up.

"That's for you," George says. His voice is unnaturally soft. "That'll be your parents."

"I just gotta finish this first."

"I'll finish it later, you go ahead."

I don't stop. My hand trembles. I press harder with the bristles, watching the paint slick itself onto the wood and soak in, filling the grain. I didn't dream about my mother in the night but upon waking that morning, before George bellowed from his own room that he was so hungry he could eat a horse and I better be awake or he'd bring a bucket of cold water to do the job, she was breathing on my face, her soft breath on my cheek like those mornings she used to come in to get me up for school and would start right in with an impossible but fantastic story. It has been a while since she's done that, but I knew if I opened my eyes just then, her freckled nose would be only inches from my own and she'd be making a silly grimace. I wanted to see her like that but I kept my eyes closed tight and blew air from my lips, blew it hard to push her out of the room. When I finally blinked she was gone.

George stands. "Go get your stuff, I'll go first."

"Fine," I say, harsher than I mean to, putting my brush down on the newspaper under the half-painted chair and running into the house through the back door. Inside, I move too fast and knock into the kitchen counter with my elbow as I race toward the stairs. "Shitfire!" I whisper, mimicking George when he swore at a baseball game on T.V. and fingering the back of my elbow as I shuffle up to the second floor. My joy at this rupture from good behavior is swift and intense. I gather my things and Lizzy, who spent the night next to me, still in the catch bucket of sea water.

When I get back downstairs I watch the three adults from behind the screen door. My mother is standing next to my dad on the parking strip. She is wearing jeans and a blue t-shirt and her hair hangs down long and straight. She has her sunglasses on her head. All three of them are talking exactly as they would on an ordinary day. I open the front door and walk slowly toward everyone, my fish bucket still in my hand.

"George says you guys caught three fish yesterday," my dad says in a voice that isn't his own.

"Three smelt." I slow my steps even further. "Just small ones."

My dad is wearing the same slacks and Huskies t-shirt I saw him in the day before when he dropped me off, but now he's no longer someone I know. George clears his throat and stares down the street.

"That's great, honey," he continues in the same odd voice. "Where did you guys go?"

I look at George to answer this question, wondering whether it would be okay to mention the ferry ride and just pretend we took the car. Usually I'm not allowed to ride his motorcycle. But George's face remains turned the wrong way.

"Did you go to the peninsula? And what's in the bucket?" he asks.

"Let's all stop being so stupid, shall we?" my mother breaks in, an easy smile on her face. Her head is tipped toward me. "I haven't even been gone that long." Then she raises her shoulders and turns to my dad, "I know, John, I should have told you where I was going, I know, I know. I didn't mean to worry you. I really didn't. But like I said, you'll never guess what I found up there."

My dad shifts on his feet, glances at me. "We'll talk about it later, honey." Then he says, "We need to let George have the rest of his day."

"Don't worry about me," George says.

But my dad shakes his head.

Then my mother continues, "It's really useful, I'll tell you all about it. We'll have to decide what to do, though, now that we know …"

"Let's just get Ella home, ok?"

She frowns at him, then, and they stare at each other for several seconds. Then she shakes her head and turns to me. She steps forward and I have to put the bucket on the ground because she's coming so close. She kneels down before me and looks me straight in the eye.

Her eyes take me in, up and down and it's a relief when she says, "You've grown three-fifths of an inch!" This is how my mother sounds when she's being silly.

She leans toward my head, "Your hair smells like my shampoo!"

Then she leans back and says, "You're going to be taller than me one day."

She reaches over and takes my right hand in her right hand, and she shakes it. Up and down, keeping us eye to eye. "Hello, Ella. I'm Maggie." She seems ready to burst out laughing, and she winks at me. But she sounds like my mother. She's gone away but here she is again. Her eyes are bright, and she's looking at me in the way that I know means she's exactly right there. She's with me. My dad and George seem far away and I shake her hand back, because we are agreeing on something, whatever that is, and I am certain I have done the right thing by taking the fish.

"So, Elly Bean," she says, her face serious. "You're safe now."

"I'm safe," I repeat. "I mean, I am?"

"Darn sure."

"Ok."

"Then it's a deal," she says.

I don't know what she means so I turn to the catch bucket and say, "This is my fish, I found her," I say. "Her name is Lizzy."

My mother leans in and whispers, although it's a loud whisper, "Ok, I get it. I can keep a secret. What kind of fish is it?"

I whisper back, confused, what does she mean by secret? "George says it's a sculpin."

She stands up, "Rock fish, right? You'll have to study her, won't you? Make careful observations."

I take in a deep breath then because I was right. I knew she'd understand. "That's my plan. And you can help me, if you want."

"I'll always help you. You know that."

But she isn't looking at me when she says it so I take her hand and squeeze her fingers, tight. Just quickly. She squeezes mine back and her eyes meet mine. I let out my breath.

11

WE LEAVE THE LAKE AND GEORGE WALKS BACK with me to my dad's house. It takes us eight minutes; we walk side by side. He holds Daisie's leash, he asks me about work, about Wenatchee, about Neil's parents whom he met a few months ago when they came to visit. It is such an ordinary conversation that it begins to trick me. I watch him from the corner of my eye—did he actually mention a cabin? Did I hallucinate this instead? Are there really photos of my mother in the bathroom drawer at my dad's house? And my nausea and tender breasts? Isn't the rest of my body sore, too? Couldn't it all just be grief and shock working their way through my body? Like an animal weak with hunger or fatigue or injury, perhaps I just need time.

The eighth minute has us walking up the driveway of my dad's house, and we have to duck to avoid a branch from the neighbor's spindly dogwood tree. Both of us lean our bodies at the same time, twist our shoulders. This tree is always hanging over the fence. Bare in winter, clouded in white flowers in spring. And in front of us, hanging askew on the garage door is the Parking for Pirates Only sign. Below it a long scratch in the beige paint. A scratch that has been there for years. I lean down to unleash the dogs and I feel it—the sensation of comfort, of here I am, of this is home. I have not lived in this house for twelve years but still it feels like home. And the lights are on behind the thin kitchen curtains, so for just a second, I can pretend.

He would greet me like this: "Elly Smelly Bean, the greatest fisherwoman in these wild northern parts."

And I would say: "Quite a compliment coming from Cap'n Johnny Fish himself, the man of 500 Chinook."

Except I cannot say this. I cannot say this to him and I cannot throw open the back door and race inside and yell, "What the fuck is this about a cabin?" I watch George, who is paused with his hand on the screen door latch, deep within the shadow of his own arrival here—is that a trembling hand, a downturned face?—and all I want to do is tack around and get the hell away from these unfamiliar waters.

We shuffle ourselves inside, the warm dry air making us blink and squint like we've emerged from some dark enclosed space. Neil is there and I cannot look at him, and the dogs zip about as we remove our coats and drop the leashes and begin to remove our shoes, and then a woman's voice comes toward me from the other room. Distinctly feminine. Throaty. Vibrant. A panic rises, can George hear this, too? But he's oblivious, still blinking furiously to clear the heat from his eyes after our walk in the cold. I twist and reach for the back door, rushing my body away from the sound. It cannot be. It simply cannot be.

But it isn't. Lisa is walking toward me, arms outstretched for an embrace; I can only choke back my absurd fear. The thought of my mother vanishes as Lisa rocks me back and forth in her arms. It has been years since her ghost has risen toward me this way. I lean over to accept Lisa's comforting, try to breathe through the edges of my residual panic. She says things like *oh, honey* and *this fucking world* and *tragedy* and *I'm sorry* and countless other meant-to-be soothing words.

"Are you alright," she says, pulling back to see my face. She isn't really asking this, so I don't need to answer.

Lisa is a talker. A hugger. Still mostly a hippie, a kind of Wiccan even. She wears her gray hair long and curly; she always smells of patchouli and marijuana. Her clothing billows around her in lengths of grays and browns and heather.

She holds my hand, tears running down her soft face. She is the best and safest kind of griever. Her own grieving will take up so much space that no one else's will matter. I press her hand in return while George walks down the hall and into the living room, then comes right back. He tries to stand with us in the kitchen, but then with only the slightest nod, he walks out into my dad's workshop in the garage.

I disentangle from Lisa and offer tea, rummage around in the cupboard for crackers or bread. Neil helps, Lisa is still talking. We sit down together in the living room where I pour the tea, I sip the tea. My stomach takes it. It even quiets for a moment. I nibble a cracker and for the first time in days my nausea takes a step back. There is such relief in this, my head clears and my heart starts racing. I sit up. Energy returning. I keep nibbling. My teeth working the cracker into dust between my lips, then washing it down with the hot tea.

Neil is telling Lisa what the surgeon told us, and she asks questions which mean George has already told her many of these same things.

"So they think it was instantaneous?"

"The angle of impact, the damage so extensive."

"And there was nothing they could have done?"

But none of us minds the repetition. We keep on this, mimicking each other, nodding, refilling our tea mugs, asking and answering the same questions. Over and over. If a pause in the conversation arises, someone quickly covers it with something we have already said.

Eventually Lisa takes over, repeating what we've all said and then she just steams right ahead. *Tragedy* and *this fucking world*. And *I'm so sorry*. At some point I realize she's talking about the last time she saw my dad.

"Such a good friend. Not just George's friend. My friend, too."

From the garage comes the sound of drawers being pulled out and closed, of cupboards being opened and shut. The whir of an empty fishing reel. I lose the thread of Lisa's talking and I see my dad again, his feet firm on the rocks, his rod held high, sunglasses and baseball hat in place, his arms working the tension in the line as he catches a bite from twenty feet below.

I come back to hear, "But also because of John and Ella's life. I don't want to consider such lovely, happy people as a tragedy." She glances at me, quickly, "Nothing about you is tragic, but you know, losing your mother like that."

I hear the thud of a pair of waders falling from their hook on the wall. The rustle of bags, of tackle.

Neil is speaking now. His careful curious tone. "Yes," he says, "But Ella doesn't consider it a tragedy. She's always been clear about that."

He knows so little of what happened. I haven't told him.

"Ella is very brave. She's had to be."

George shuffles into the room. His nose is red. His shoulders down. He sits down on the arm of the couch.

"It's good to be here," she says, placing a hand on his leg. "It's good for us to sit here together."

George *humnphs*, his gruff self while Lisa keeps on. This is what she does, bringing people into her warmth. "We need to be together. We need to talk about John, and his life." She turns to me then, eyes wide and soft. "Ella, we were talking last night about the photos."

I nod like I'm willing to talk about this, but I gather up our empty tea cups and go into the kitchen. Ghost ships always invite the curious thrill seekers. But they're really just dead wood. All good sailors know this. There is never any sunken treasure.

I hear George clear his throat. Neil will have sat up a bit. I stay in the kitchen. I will make more hot water. I will pour more tea. I rinse our tea cups and pot.

Neil says, "Did you know about Ella's mom? I mean, what do you think?"

George says something but I don't hear it. Then Neil responds. I turn off the water. Stand perfectly still.

The pitch of George's voice means that his hands are twitching; he's nervous. "And then she left. I know that John might have gotten some information about her once or twice. This was early on. But then nothing after that. She was just gone."

Yes, I think. Go on, George, tell them that she was just gone.

"How old do you think she is in the photos from John's wallet?" This from Lisa.

"I just think John would have told me. And now this weird thing about the cabin. That doesn't make any sense."

"A cabin?" Neil's voice is louder now.

"Up on Hat Island. Ella didn't know about it. It's a small place. I assumed you two had been up there."

This was lucky, Cap'n Johnny. Not keeping this cabin from George, but keeping it from me.

"Wait, you're saying John had a cabin. We didn't know about this. Did Ella know about this? You've been there?" Neil's voice is hushed, surprised.

"A couple times. Spent the night so we could be out at Wilkinson for the dawn run of Blackmouth."

"When's the last time you went?"

"Two, three months ago."

Lisa's voice is calm, curious, "So this cabin might have something to do with Maggie?"

"How?" says Neil.

"I just mean if they were in touch again. Maybe she lives there?"

How quickly the world splits. But George breaks in, "No, no. I went there. It's a fishing cabin. It's really small. No one was living there. I'm sure."

My hands shake as I pour the hot water into the tea pot.

"But anyway," George continues. "It doesn't make sense. John just wouldn't."

And here I agree with George. My dad just wouldn't. None of this—he just wouldn't. I put the tea pot onto the tray, wipe the palms of my hands against my jeans. Try to calm the tremor in them.

Lisa breaks in, calls for me. "Ella, honey, come back here, can we talk about this?"

Of course we can talk about this. I put four mugs on the tray and walk back into the room.

I hand around the mugs and I'm already talking, "We need to contact St. Mark's. I meant to do it first thing today, but now that I think about it, I'm worried the church won't be big enough."

Everyone stares at me.

George says, "Maybe he told you and you forgot? Maybe this isn't anything important." He pauses, then, "Ella, surely he told you."

Neil's brow furrows, "But I would have known."

"Think about it," I say. "The entire ferry service. That's a lot of people. And neighbors, too. St. Mark's is kind of a small church."

"Ella?" this from Lisa, her face grave. "I know this is hard. I know you don't want to talk about your mother."

I blink and meet her gaze. I am extremely calm.

"But this is the time," she says, and her face grows emotional with her idea. "I mean, really, I've never liked the hush hush about everything. I told John that. I've always told John it wasn't good you never talked about it."

George shushes her gently but it's no use.

"That woman," she says. "That woman caused so many problems. I know I wasn't around when it all happened, but you've said enough," she looks at George, who is looking at his hands, a deep frown on his face. "I've heard enough to know that, frankly, you two," she is looking at me now, "were lucky she left. I'm not saying it wasn't sad—of course it was sad—and I'm not saying it wasn't tragic, well, tragic for her."

I don't know what she says after this because I have reached for the hot teapot with my bare hands, have picked it up, palms flat on the burning porcelain. I have to drop it, throw it away from my skin. It smashes to the floor, and hot tea splashes high. "I'm so sorry!" I yell, already racing into the kitchen for tea towels while everyone swipes at their arms and clothes, tries to mop up the spill with napkins and tissues.

"Let me see your hands," Neil says.

I show him, palms up. I'm not really burned, but I go and run cold water over my fingertips in the upstairs bathroom because Lisa has gone into the downstairs one to rinse a tea stain from the sleeve of her shirt.

I let the water run and run because I know that George has to get to work. I shout downstairs and I hope this will be enough but Lisa comes upstairs anyway, sticks her head through the door and says, "Come by later, I'll cook for you."

"Thank you," I say, but I know we won't do this. I keep my fingers under the cold water.

"It's best to talk about these things, my lovey. Don't hold it in. We can take it. We can help you."

I nod at her. Just go, I'm thinking. Just please fucking go.

And she finally does. I keep my fingers under the water until they're pink with cold, and then I dry them, standing, staring at my reflection in the sink. I am not her. I am not her. She does not exist. She left. She was gone. I know this is true. There is only one thing to do. I take my cell phone out of my pocket, I search for the number of the gynecologist I had when I still lived in Seattle. I dial and let it ring, then I hang up. But I call back and before I can think about it, I make an appointment for three days later. I will need a blood test. I will need to be sure. The tea and crackers have kept my nausea at bay but I don't feel quite right. My body is trying to tell me something but I don't know what it is. When I hang up I sit perfectly still and I concentrate, think and settle and listen, and I evaluate the state of the animal in my presence. But it doesn't work, this animal isn't giving anything away.

I can hear Neil in the kitchen downstairs and so I walk into my dad's den, shut the door behind me. Everything in this room is about boats—the prints on the walls, the paperweights and pencil holders. On the shelf is his collection of books about The Graveyard of the Pacific, that harrowing strip of ocean that has claimed something like 2000 boats since people started keeping track. He loved studying this history, and so I know he's the only one who might know what to do; he knows all about the perils and depths of the sea. I am remembering how he loved to sail up past the Columbia Bar, telling me how difficult it was to navigate safely. How many times did we do this? I see us watching for boats, for waves, looking for safe harbor.

I get up from his desk and step across the hall to his bedroom. I do not turn on the light. I stand in the doorway and hold my breath until

I think I'm ready to confront the scent of this room. When I dare to breathe in—this wonderful, horrible, familiar scent—it fills me and it stops me, and I back away because it's like a presence, and within it, it is impossible for me to believe that he is gone. So I choose not to believe it. Just for a moment. I step forward, sucking the air deep into my lungs, and I close my eyes and stretch my hands out in front of me. I circle the room, fumbling against the furniture and guessing at objects I touch. Photograph frames, a stack of dusty paperbacks, a handkerchief, a deck of cards, a miniature ferryboat ornament on the dresser. I imagine that I can come across my dad in this rustling around, imagine that he's sitting here waiting for me and will shout, "Got ya!" and the whole of what has happened will be nothing but a cruel joke.

Within minutes my nose assimilates what surprised it a moment ago. I sit down on the bed and I open my eyes. He is no longer here. And I'm not sure anymore who he was. What's the trade for this? I can't find one anywhere. The room is completely empty. I punch the pillow. My fist flies into the dented space where my dad's head is meant to be resting. I've never in my life considered hitting him but here it is. And the fact that he isn't here to receive the blow does not alter how good it feels to want to commit this violence against him. So I punch him again and again, smashing the surface of the cotton, changing the shape of his indent, fighting at this empty space until I have changed it, until I have transformed it into something I have made with my own two hands.

12

THE THING ABOUT HEELING IS THAT THERE'S a point when you go too far, when the only possible outcome is to capsize. When I was in middle school I wrote a report on capsize risks for fishing trawlers. My teacher was very impressed. It was both a vocabulary study and a math lesson. She gave me an A+. She called my dad to tell him how well I was doing. That she was sure I'd be fine, despite all the trouble, because I kept my head at school, did my work.

I was careful though. Because capsize risks are really hard to determine precisely. You've got to work out the stability curve, which is the angle the boat can heel and still right itself. You don't want to push things too far, in other words. You want reserve buoyancy because that's the way to get through the waves and the wind.

After, sailing up past the Columbia Bar all those times, my dad taught me about this. He showed me how we could let the wind roll us, let the waves rock us. Mostly because our boat was a good one, but also because we were a crew that knew what it was doing.

"The vertical center of gravity really can't be low enough," he said.

"And gas tanks must be baffled or filled," I answered, because I knew he'd smile at me then.

"Keep heavy items low to deck," he said.

"And no oversized rigging up high," I said.

That's how we sailed so smoothly. We only had to discuss the external conditions—wind speed and wave height, wave direction—and keep our boat righted.

"Don't ever forget," my dad said. "When a wave crest hits your topsides, it gives the energy that will start your boat heeling."

"Don't I know it, Captain," I said. Once the wave has passed there is nothing you can do about it. You can't look back. It's gone anyway. Waves vanish like that. No two waves are the same. So hunker low. Look forward. Point your boat. Keep sailing.

13

"Here," Neil says, his arm outstretched as he walks into my dad's room a few hours later. I haven't moved from the bed; my hand rests on the flattened pillow. I close my eyes then open them quickly, hoping he will hand me something extraordinary. I'm hoping for a stone—a thunder egg, a smoky quartz, an agate. Something from his usual hoard of treasures. Maybe one he gave my dad once that he's just come across on a shelf.

Instead, he places the letter into my palm. An ordinary letter. I sit up. "Just look at this, Ella."

It has been so long but I recognize it right away. How dare she, I think, with a burst of energy. My feet come down with a thump on the hardwood floor. Show me how to unfurl the sails, Captain.

"Do you want to come and see? There are a whole bunch of them."

But instead of answering, I push back the sliding door to my dad's closet, take the deepest breath I have ever taken in my life and step inside. I take another step, right in between the hanging clothes. A metal hanger brushes my cheek, cool and sharp.

I raise a coat sleeve to my face. Let the fabric touch my cheek. I squeeze myself behind the rows of hanging suits and sports jackets. It's dark in the closet and cramped but I have enough room behind the clothes to move around. I duck, slip my hand into the pocket of one of the coats and pull out a wadded Kleenex and a nickel. I put them in my own pocket and reach for another coat. Its pockets are empty so I try another. And another.

Neil stands at the closet door. "Ella?"

My voice is a whisper when it comes. "Second drawer down in the green filing cabinet? In a large manila envelope?"

Through the hanging clothes I see him open his mouth, then close it before speaking.

I test each of my dad's pants' pockets, messing up their neat arrangement on the hangers. I lean over to the floor and reach inside his shoes, pull back their tongues and shove their laces inside. I push past a few more sweaters and find my dad's old winter coat.

Neil sighs, reaches a long arm out, pushes some of my dad's clothing aside and joins me in the closet. A t-shirt falls to the floor.

Of course my mother's letters are still in the house, are still exactly where my dad once kept them. That one drawer, unremarkable from the others in the tiny room off the garage that my dad has for storing paperwork and files. A place I used to tiptoe into as a teenager, to reach for that drawer, to pull my arm back again and retreat. Tiptoe away. This was one of the pacts I made with my mother. I promised not to think about her, to let her go because that is what she asked of me.

"We'll have to give all of this away," I say.

"You knew they were writing to each other?"

"No," I say, more curtly then I mean to, pressing a hand down the thick wool of my dad's old coat and scrambling for an answer. Not the real answer, but some kind of answer. "They never wrote to each other. That isn't from her."

"What do you mean?"

What *do* I mean? I mean that I was eleven when the letters first started to come. That I would see them before my dad, that I would slip them beneath the rest of the mail and hold everything tightly pressed and hidden until I was safely inside the house. "I mean that would have been too easy, wouldn't it?" I say. "That would have changed everything."

"Ella?"

"She left, Neil. She left when I was ten and she never came back. We never found out what happened to her. We were better off without her."

He says nothing, and I reach into a box and find a stack of coiled belts. Obviously ones my dad hasn't been able to wear for some time.

"You told me that before. But I didn't know about letters." He pulls some sweaters from the upper shelf. "I can do this for you. You don't have to."

I say nothing. I'm too busy resisting the urge to put my dad's shirts on, one on top of the other. I'm holding the sleeves and wondering how to get out of this closet. Except that I never want to leave this closet.

Neil is refolding the sweaters, putting them back on the high shelf. I stop his hands, take two of the sweaters in my arms and hug them.

"Ella, love, what does it mean that she was writing to you? Or to your dad?"

"I'm saying these weren't from her." I take a deep breath, nearly a sigh, because I know what to do now. It is easy to explain how After worked. I've never been in any doubt about this. "You have to realize that our address and phone number were listed with the national missing person association—that means anyone could contact us, even people who were missing. It's something that happens. It's horrible for the families."

"This is what your dad explained to you?"

I shake past the thought that my dad didn't explain much. Talking about it was too hard. I was very young. "This is what I knew. What we knew. Sometimes we would get these letters, from people claiming to be my mother, or even not."

He shakes his head. He doesn't believe me. I push the dress shirts aside. One by one. Trying to make a space on the hanging rod.

"Are you looking for something specific?" he says quietly.

I don't answer. I won't find my dad in here. I know this, but I can't seem to step away.

"Ella?"

I pick up a fallen hanger. Find a button on the floor.

"Why don't we go downstairs?" The letter is still in his hand, crumpling now.

"You don't have to help me."

"Ella?"

"Have you even read it?"

"Just quickly."

"Read it again. You'll see what I mean." This is a gamble, but it works.

He opens the folded page, scans it, passes it over to me. A feeling like triumph ignites as I read her loopy handwriting, see the messy ink splotches:

I don't approve of alerts or milk cartons. I didn't INVENT these concepts and anyone using "identity" as a means to safety must be a thief or A PRETENDER himself. We're talking about the most at-risk. Identity system for "theft," relay and safe house system for "theft," social work care system for "theft." No harm must be done.

The letter is signed "Margot". But this is half-crossed out, followed by the letters M-A-R written carefully three times. "You see," I lie. "This was just some random person who found our address."

Neil puts a hand to the back of his head, then brings it forward and rubs his eyes. "It doesn't make any sense. Don't you know what happened to her? And what did your dad do about these letters?"

I shrug, I shake my head. "We lived without her. That's what we had to do."

"Did he follow them up? Go looking for her?"

I shake my head. "She left us. That's all we ever needed to know."

Neil drops his hands, lets out a deep sigh. His voice is very careful. "I'm so sorry, Ella. I'm sorry you're having to think about this again. But I still don't understand. Was she sick? What really happened?"

How quickly the world splits. How hard it is to put back together, to make it seamless again. Neil isn't supposed to see any of this. I'm fine now and he shouldn't have to worry. I just want us to ignore her. "It's like this, Neil," I begin, and I'm going to make it clear once and for all that there is nothing interesting in bringing this all up again. That it was all so long ago. "I appreciate how much you want to understand. But that's the thing of it. There isn't anything to understand. What happened was simple. She left. We were on our own. We made it."

Two lines appear between Neil's eyes. He tips his head. "I think …" But he stops, rubs his forehead with his fingers. "I think this is really hard for you."

I say nothing. I turn my attention to my dad's dress shirts and press the flat of my hand against their equally flat breast pockets. I touch the flannel shirts twice. Neil takes a deep breath. Then another.

I find my dad's old jogging clothes—gym shorts and frayed sweatshirts. I start to pull these out and throw them into a pile in the middle of the room.

"Stop," Neil says. But I don't. So he reaches for a suit in a plastic sheath. "Is this his uniform?"

"Don't touch that," I say.

Neil keeps a hold of the zipper and speaks slowly. "Tell me what you want so I can help."

"You're wrinkling it!" I try to snatch it from him.

"I'm not."

"You're letting it crease on the floor!"

He hands it over. It's an old uniform. I doubt he's worn it in a few years. Still, I unzip the plastic sheath. Force myself to keep my eyes open in the face of all that stark white cloth. Then I place it back into its rightful place, smoothing my hands across the shoulders on the hanger. My dad was never this short. To hug him I had to practically jump into the air, reach up despite my own long legs. I slump against the back wall, pull my knees into my chest. And still I want to howl at the sheer genius of death. How perfectly fucking final and unarguable it is.

"You see," I say.

"No," Neil says, sliding down to sit beside me. He places a hand on my leg. "I mean, this is hard for you to see differently. It's like you've decided how it all went."

"There's nothing to see differently. And it was a really long time ago now."

"You've decided you know what happened. But that can't be true anymore. I wish we could ask your dad, but we can't. We're going to have to look into it."

A muscle tightens in my throat. Why would my dad not tell me if he knew where she was? It doesn't make any sense. We both decided. I put a hand to massage my neck. I'm about to refute Neil's statement but from the den comes the sound of the phone ringing and we have to shift ourselves from out behind my dad's clothes and leave the closet. I am pulling on one of my dad's old wool hats as I take the phone in my dad's den. It's the funeral home. A woman informs me that this afternoon would be perfect.

"Perfect," I repeat.

She coughs and says, "What I mean is that we can accommodate your schedule of course, just let me know when you can come by."

Which is immediately, because this is a chance to see my dad's body. I don't need to sit in the bottom of his closet or put on all of his shirts one by one and test his shoes. I will be able to sit with him, just for a moment, and maybe this will tell me about the kind of man he was and if his secret can fit in the same room with the two of us together.

We find his current uniform in the downstairs closet and we call George at work, figure out when he can leave, arrange who will drive, put the dogs out, and then before too long we're all driving north together to Swann's funeral home.

It takes us twenty minutes to get there, and we don't speak. We turn off the road in front of a large, stone house. The building is gray, the window awnings striped gray and white. It's an ugly structure. In the parking lot, George is visibly nervous and pulls out a cigarette before we get to the door. He asks me if I'm ready, he asks Neil if he knows what to expect. "I've been to viewings before, it isn't easy," he says.

Careful gruff George. Of course he's worried about this. I say nothing, watch him smoke furiously. I think of how my job has somehow prepared me for this, how it was something I learned to get over.

Then, with a chill, I hug the sleeves of my winter coat and remember how in the early years of working at the clinic I'd had dreams of euthanized animals getting back up off the table and speaking to me in my mother's voice.

"Come on," I say, trying to be gentle but I sound too impatient and must swallow the words because George isn't quite done smoking and Neil has stopped to wait for him.

"Catholics used to hold the viewing at home," George says, finally walking up the steps of the gray house. "For several days."

"I wouldn't like that," says Neil.

Then, finally, both men are shuffling forward, climbing the last of the steps and bracing their shoulders, readying themselves for what we are going to see.

But this isn't what happens at all. We make it up the steps, cross the threshold of this somber building and enter a hall with silk flowers, careful urns and dully bright commemorative plates. We introduce ourselves to the young female funeral director. But then one moment I am preparing myself to be in the same room again with my dad, and the next the woman is explaining that there has been some mistake.

"This has never happened in all the years my parents and grandparents ran the business," she explains, her eyes jumping between the three of us. "So I have no idea how to handle this except to give you my sincerest apologies." She takes a deep breath. "The hospital gave us the information that your father was not presentable. I'm sorry to be the one to tell you this, they should have done that. I didn't realize you ..." here she looks to George and Neil, back and forth.

My dad will not be presentable, I think, like someone has spilled soup on his clothing, or a glass of wine across his white captain's uniform.

"I didn't realize," she continues, "until one of you called yesterday, that you hadn't seen him." Suddenly she stops wringing her hands and straightens. "I can confirm that a viewing would not have been appropriate based on Mr. Tomlinson's injuries."

"What kind of mistake?" Neil asks.

"What exactly are you telling us?" George says. "We don't want a public viewing at the ceremony. Today is for us."

But I understand right away that my dad has already been cremated. I sit down on one of the suede sofas and blink at the funeral director. She is wearing a charcoal gray pantsuit. Her hair is swept back. She is as tall as I am and I wonder if this helps her in this kind of work. I just keep staring at her. Of all things, my anger has nowhere to go. I wanted to see his face. I wanted to have him in my presence as if that would have somehow held him accountable.

"I'm so sorry," the director repeats. "We arranged for you to pick up your dad's ashes today."

"Where is he, then?" I ask. It is not what I mean to say but she seems to understand me. She invites us into a second room. She closes the door behind us. Neil and George walk beside me. George's face is red, his hands balled into fists inside his jacket. Neil is bowed, turned toward me.

She brings me a box and I slip a dark gray cardboard sheaf off the plastic box and open it, only to find just another box inside.

When I turn to her, not understanding, the woman whispers, "Ashes are very fine. This is a kind of protection. It keeps everything together."

But nothing is together, I want to say. Nothing about this day or about this box has anything to do with being together. I open the final box with fumbling fingers. They are fine, very fine and unevenly colored like gradations of wet to dry sand on a beach. My dad would have said this, it is his voice in my ears making this remark. I've seen ashes before, many times, always in the context of my job—dog and cat ashes, other animals—but there is just so much this time. More ashes than I could have imagined. And yet it is all of my quiet giant of a dad, reduced to this little square box.

14

SHE'S AT THE KITCHEN TABLE MOST MORNINGS now. And most afternoons. This is July of that last summer. And I'm to leave her alone because my dad keeps saying that she needs rest, that she's still recovering from the flu and pretty worn out. It isn't too hard to stay out of her way. I know how to keep busy, work on my science project or watch TV. But this afternoon she looks up from the kitchen table when I come in to get a Popsicle from the freezer. Her eyes focus in on me and she jerks her head back, like she's surprised to see me. Just for a second. Then she draws herself up and says, "Your fish is turning green. There's something wrong with the water."

"I'm changing the pump today," I say. Quiet, no sass. "And she changes color like that. It's her special trick."

"There's no one else here. You don't have to worry."

"I'm not worried."

"Then why are you whispering?"

"I'm not," I say.

She drops her pen then, in an angry way, and I explain that she's right, Lizzy is maybe sick and I was just going to check the mail to see if the new pump is there. I tell her that Lizzy has been hanging around at the bottom of her tank—no jumps, no gliding along. I ask her if she wants to help me change the pump.

She's rubbing her temples. She takes a deep breath. "Anyway, your dad's out. God knows where."

"He's covering for Bill," I say. "He told me last night. He said he left you a note." And like every morning now, he also told me exactly what time he'd be home and to call him at the pier if I needed anything. I told him not to worry. I told him, "Clear seas, Captain."

"Oh well, that's just what he said," my mother says then.

"It's true what he said." I can't stop the note of pleading from entering my voice. She never believes my dad anymore. She's always calling him a liar. But she's the one who makes things up. She's the one who tells stories that aren't true.

"A lot of things may be true," she says, now rubbing her forehead. "But that isn't what matters. True is what we think will save us. But that's just hope." She picks up the pen and clicks it twice. "And that's probably not going to be enough."

She shifts in her seat, is focusing again on her writing, her notebook, and I know that if I keep really still she might forget about me. She's wearing a dress that I love, one she made for herself out of a purple fabric with tiny white sailboats. She made me one, too. Years before. But I've grown out of it. It strikes me then that it isn't just children who grow up and out of their clothes. My mother doesn't fit her dress anymore. Not the size. The person. She's wearing this dress that has been hers, but she isn't herself. I start to back away.

But she clicks her pen again and says, "Maybe you can take it."

I wait. I know I just have to wait.

"There's so much to explain," she continues. "And it's hard to know how much I can tell you. You're not a little girl anymore. But you're not grown up yet, either."

"I'm ten, Mom."

"What?" Again, she raises a hand to her face. Tips her head at me.

"I'm ten," I repeat. She is staring at me.

"Of course I know that. Why are you telling me that? There's no need to repeat everything."

I say nothing. She looks just like my mother—her wide green eyes, the line of her mouth, those slender fingers. But she isn't my mother. I don't know who she is and all I want to know is how I can get away from her.

"I'm going ..." I start but she isn't listening.

"Hey, do you want to help me with something?" She waves me toward the table. "Come on."

"I just have to change the pump on Lizzy's tank," I say. "Then I have to work on my project."

She shrugs, her smile tight. "I don't want to scare you. But this is more important."

There are ripped papers and newspapers and pencils spread out on the table. Scissors and an open glue stick.

"I have to work on my Lizzy project."

Her smile falls, her face darkens. "What you need to know here is vital. I mean it, Ella. More than your science project."

"Okay," I say quickly. "Okay."

She smiles then. "I want you to write exactly what I've written here," she says, thrusting a sheet of white paper in front of me. "I need to send a lot of these letters out but I can't use a Xerox because they would think I wasn't serious. It has to be handwritten."

I nod, sit down at the table across from her, and reach for a pen.

"Not that one. We both have to write in blue."

I take the blue pen she holds out to me.

"You can write just like me? It has to be identical."

"I don't know."

"You can," she says, her eyes closing halfway. "Anyway, I'll check it when you're done."

And then she sits down with her pen and another sheet of paper and is already writing.

I scoot my chair to the left. I try reading the letter she's left for me to copy but the words are swimming, my eyes are watering, so I tell myself to stop being such a baby. She is writing fast, scribbling. Her handwriting will be very difficult to copy. There are a lot of questions in the body text of the letter, some of them even marked with multiple question marks. *Proper procedure is important,* one sentence reads, *so is identifying the risks from all angles??* And farther down the page, *If we can't trust the school system to keep our children safe, then who can we trust? This is a matter that bears careful scrutiny.* I don't know what "scrutiny" means, and I don't understand what the letter is trying to say. I read it and read it, wondering who it's for. But then I stop reading it.

"Hurry up," she says. "We need about twenty of these."

I move the piece of paper in front of me, I hold the pen over the blank sheet and make a show of reading the model letter again carefully. But my mouth has gone dry. My legs begin to prickle with the need to get up and move. She has misspelled several words. Easy words. Words like "comming" and "ignor"; and she's repeated others, like two "the's" about halfway down the page. She's written "an bridge" instead of "a bridge." Has she done this on purpose? I start copying out the letter.

"Remember, I always loop my l's—you can do that, right?"

I nod. I listen to the scratching of her pen on the paper, listen to how furiously she's writing. This is not how she usually writes. She's usually a careful person. She usually has small, neat handwriting that spools off the end of the pen. Today her hands are chapped and ink-stained. A paper cut bleeds on her knuckle and she licks it from time to time. I glance at the model letter again, at those misspellings and the smudges of ink. At the way the lines tilt. I know I will have to write fast to mimic her. To make the same kind of messy fast handwriting. I try for a few sentences, but it doesn't work. So I carefully fold my first paper and tuck it onto my lap. Grab another one.

I check the clock. Again and again, I check the clock. I am thinking that I have to be really careful. There's no way around it even if my dad should be home fairly soon.

So I write quickly, as quickly as I can, looping my l's and making those same spelling mistakes. When I finish the letter I turn it face down on the table and take another piece of paper. My mother is still writing. She's on her fourth letter. She's said we need to do about twenty of them.

She checks on me and I nod at her. Show her that I'm writing quickly, like she wants me to. I keep my face still. Concentrate on the task she's given me. She doesn't get up to check my letter and I let out the breath I'm holding. Finish my second letter and flip that one over too, then start on a third. And while I write, I keep hoping that my dad will come home before we reach twenty. Before we reach twenty she will get up to check my letters.

This is sometime in late July. When we all still lived in the country of Before. But this is the last day that everyone will pretend that everything is really fine and that all my dad has to do is tell me when he's coming home, tell me to keep a bit out of her way. Because by the time my dad does come home, my mother has checked all my letters and she's holding my hand for me, helping me, writing the letters with me instead of next to me, and we are on letter number 36 and she's broken my pinky finger by accident, just by squeezing my hand a little too hard.

15

THAT EVENING A STORM MOVES ITS WAY across the city—rolling in from the ocean and up over the hills of the neighborhood. Lightning flashes across the rooftops; I stand at the guest room window and watch the rain fall in sheets across the swathe of yellow light cast by the street lamp. Cars dart in and out of driveways and garages. Neighbors return home and scurry inside their houses. I know the ocean will be rough, the winds high. The ferries will be operating carefully this evening. The captains and crews on alert. I wait to feel sleepy but it never comes. An hour passes. Then another. Neil comes in and out of the room, watches the storm with me. Trapp sits at my side, just as attentive.

This is grief, they must be thinking.

This is grief, I tell myself.

At some point we get undressed and we align our bodies in the bed with our eyes closed. I don't expect to but I fall into a deep sleep for two or three hours. Then I wake with the memory of a dream in which I am holding half an animal in each hand. In the dream it doesn't bother me that this animal has been sliced in half, what is bothering me is that I cannot tell what kind of animal it is. I keep turning each hand and trying to find a face or a paw or a tail, something to indicate whether this is a cat or a small dog, a squirrel or something else entirely.

I rub the palms of my hand against the sheets, trying to remove the feeling of slick fur and blood. My stomach turns. I can still smell the dead animal's innards. I shake myself out of the dream fog and get up, go to the bathroom and drink some water. My face in the mirror is too thin, my skin tight and dry, my hair wild. I quickly braid it, tame it. I slip downstairs—quietly, quickly—which is at first just something to do instead of go back to bed, but when I walk into the small storage room and reach for the first file drawer I know this is why I've woken up. No matter the animal, I will not just leave it. An animal cannot be left to die in two distinct parts, it's my job to sew it all back together no matter how futile, no matter how much blood has been lost.

And it isn't even hard to find. My dad keeps his files organized, orderly. Handwritten tabs stretch back through the drawer—*HOUSE, TRUCK, Bank of A*, just like that. Between the mortgage and insurance papers for the house, I find the deed to a small cabin on Hat Island, a residence permit, and a boat slip rental receipt. It's all filed away for me, perfectly reasonable. Like it wasn't a secret, like I was supposed to know about it all along. The deed is in both of their names. I blink on it. It isn't possible.

Because just the other day he said, "Harbor seals."

And he said, "What species are you up so early for?"

He did not say, not once, not ever, "I bought a small cabin on Hat Island six years ago with your mom and never told you."

"Clear seas, Captain?" I whisper.

A whisper answers me, "Watch out for whales."

I whirl around to an empty doorway. Close my eyes. Shut my ears. I do not want this—the ease with which I can imagine it all, conjure up a person, a reason, an idea. This is what she did. My heart skitters and my hands are shaking, but I breathe through it. I count the seconds. Beat one. Beat two. Beat three. Beat four. I catalog the physical items in this room: the shelves, the boxes, the rolled up maps against the wall. This is a real filing cabinet, a real room, I am a real person. The papers in my hands have weight and texture. These are impossible facts.

How I have loved this phrase over the years. I see myself—white-coated and arrogant in my educated compassion—telling a client about the impossible facts: the growth of malignant tissue in a matter of days, the inexplicable expression of a genetic disorder in an otherwise healthy animal, the first-time occurrence of wayward and disastrous behavior. I've hidden behind these two words like they might actually mean something or they might help.

But now these ownership papers in my hand. With their impossible dates and names. It can't be possible. George said so, too. Said that no one lives there. My dad just wouldn't.

My fingers walk across the labels on the file folders. Nothing is in alphabetical order, my dad was organized but not methodical: *INSURANCE, ELLA SCHOOL*, his boat under *GINZ*, and then between *LEGAL* and *WSDOT* is a file called *KEEP* and I pull it out and place it on my lap. I open it right away.

Inside the file are medical records. Receipts and charts and notes. For a patient named Maggie Tomlinson. I have to read everything twice to understand even if it's all actually quite simple. At some point a Jane Doe checked into a hospital in Oregon, my dad was somehow, miraculously located, and Maggie Tomlinson checked out. But not before receiving bone grafts, blood transfusions, weeks of physical therapy. She was in a serious accident. A crushed femur. She must have been nearly unable to walk. I find my dad's signature across many of these papers and hunt for dates. When did this happen? When did he visit her in the hospital? When did he go through all of this without telling me? And why not tell me?

I flip back and find the earliest date, discover that he rescued Jane Doe six years before taking the cabin. And just like this a six-year lie becomes a twelve-year lie. I do the math. I was eighteen when he found her. I may have still been living in this house.

I must have cried out because Trapp is immediately at my side, nosing my leg. I put the file down and keep my hand on his head, pressing and smoothing at his ears. He tries to lick my hand, something he never does, so I know I must be shaking.

No, she ran a chute on us—I know she did. And yes, my dad and I were stuck in that dog-hole, but we knew how to get out of it. We held steady in the veer of the wind. We got into the clear and then we made our boat as seakindly as possible. No wave too big, no wind too strong.

Captain? Where's the bearing? Where's the same-side object?

There are steps at the door way, and Neil's voice. "Ella?"

I close myself around these papers but I'm too late. Neil walks into the room, wanting to see what I'm doing, wanting to help and understand.

"Please, El. Let me look at all of this with you. Tell me what it's all about."

"Okay, okay," I say. I take a breath. "No, it's okay." I don't stop him when he takes the papers. "I know what it is."

Neil stares.

"All I can figure is that we were just using opposite prefixes."

"What?" Neil furrows his brow as he reads the papers. His eyes are wide, he says, "This is her?" He reads carefully, but I put a hand out across the file and stop him.

"Don't you see, we were using opposite prefixes. He must have had the danger sighted on starboard and I kept it on port. So, of course."

Neil looks at me, looks at his papers. Shakes his head. "This means that she nearly died. This is incredible. It's amazing they found your dad."

And then, "So this cabin, in her name, too …"

"Yes," I say, pushing around the angry, testing the surface of my sad. "It's just another trade."

"Ella, look at this."

Don't say, look, Neil. Don't ever ask me to *look*.

But he's reading again, he's going over the deed to the cabin. "My God, Ella, you don't want me to, but I'm starting to understand. Your dad wouldn't lie just to lie. There has to be some explanation. I mean, this whole thing is crazy. What if she does live there?"

"No, she can't. And George said …"

He looks up at me and I see it now, the pity. He's starting to understand so I shake my head. I refuse it.

"No, Neil," I say, "We're heeling, can't you feel it? And I'm not sure I can right us after all."

16

I WANT TO TELL THIS TEN-YEAR-OLD GIRL in my memory to get up from the floor. To close the window and leave this bedroom. To leave the house. Instead, she keeps at it—shoulders tense, eyes fixed—watching. This is the best view onto the back yard and I've been stationed at it for the last twenty minutes this August morning. I'm wriggling my fingers while I crouch at the sill, thumb to pinky, thumb to pinky. The doctor has told me to work it like this, each day, to strengthen the joint that was snapped. It rained in the night and the window sill is damp, the glass a bit foggy. I'm a bit shivery in my pajamas, but I can't seem to move. Below me is my mother's beautiful garden—her tomatoes and dahlias, her sunflowers and zucchinis and green beans—but it's a total wreck. All the plants have been dug up and tossed into a pile. She must have done this hard labor in the night, and now she's just working the details, on her knees in the bare soil. She has a trowel in her hand and is plunging it deep into the earth, bringing up a load of dirt and scattering it back into place with her free hand.

My dad is beside her, crouched down in the light drizzle. From my angle above him, he looks so small. I flex my fingers again, thumb to pinky. He raises a hand to his head and says something that is too quiet for me to hear. Then my mother stands up, throws the trowel across the garden and yells, "Oh, come on, John!" I duck down, I nearly fall, and I watch them with only half of my eyes over the window sill.

He stands and shakes his head, holds out his hand like he's going to give her something, but she just gets angrier. "Don't think I don't know what you're doing!"

My dad says something, but my mother cuts him off, "Speak normally!"

"I am!" my dad yells. It's such a shock to hear his voice raised and I pull it deep inside me where it starts a small fire. I'm angry, too.

"That was yelling!"

"Jesus, Maggie, you're the one yelling! You are the one who's always yelling!"

Yes, I think. Tell her, I think.

"Don't manipulate me. I know what you're doing."

"What *I'm* doing?" my dad says, tipping his head back and throwing his arms up to the gray sky. In my perch over the garden, I do the same and my arms are electric and strong. "What *I'm* doing?" He gestures at the garden, at the mess of it, and the hand at the end of his arm shakes. "Just tell me what you're doing! Please! For God's sake!"

My mother takes a step away from him. "Stop bullying me!"

He freezes. I freeze, too. His hands are still extended toward her but he pulls them back and quickly covers his face while I watch his tall body quake and I hear him take in the deepest breath I've ever heard. I take one in, too, shaking, because she's the bully. My mother stands there watching him, and then she says, "Anyway, I have so much to do. You're not helping me at all."

He loses it then, and a mournful wail rises up out of his body as he dips down and hoists a great armful of the garden debris at his feet. "I'll help you," he bellows, hurling the debris at the garage wall while I sit above them, furious, excited.

"Stop it!" she yells. "Stop!"

"No! Because someone has to clean up your fucking crazy messes!" Then he takes another armful and another, throwing each pile, grunting each time he launches one away from him.

I scurry out of their room and back to my own. Stand in the center of my carpet and I'm so jittery I can hardly contain myself. My dad never gets upset. His face never gets red. His voice never trembles. We're not just waiting and watching. We're not just afraid. I get dressed in clean summer clothes, limbs tight, body contained, staring into the greenish light of Lizzy's fish tank because it gives me somewhere to focus. School is starting in a few weeks and my project isn't working. I strain my ears into the house and beyond. Nothing inside. Nothing outside. My fish floats listlessly near the bottom of the tank. She's gotten so much worse. What are we going to do?

The back door slams and I freeze. But then my dad calls me from the bottom of the stairs. "Ella?"

"I'm up!" I yell, running down to meet him in the kitchen.

He's clutching his white hat and twirling it—two times, three times, tension in his hands. His face is white, his mouth a tight line. "I've switched with Don, so I can be back at 2:00 PM, but now I'm really late and we need to race so I can drop you at Sonja's on my way."

I shake my head. If he's taking Don's run, he needs to be at the Pier in fifteen minutes. "That will make you even more late. I can go on my own."

We stare at each other. He looks at his watch and I know he won't make it. We both know. Captain's cannot be late. The whole day's schedule will be off. Still he says, "I'm taking you to Sonja's."

"It's okay," I say, and I mean it, because we're not afraid anymore. I stand tall. "You can't, Dad. I will walk by myself. I promise." We're quiet for just a fraction of a second and then I ask, "She's outside?"

My dad looks down and I pull my hands behind me to hide my still-bandaged pinky. He says, "She's walked to the nursery for something. I don't know what."

"Ok, I'll hurry. I'll leave in ten minutes. I promise."

"Eight minutes," he says, pulling the keys from his pocket. "Then call me when you get to Sonja's. I'll be back here at two." He pauses. "You know you can always radio for me on the boat, if ever you need me."

I salute him. "Aye, aye, Captain."

He smiles but it doesn't reach his eyes. He glances at George's telephone number magneted to the fridge before walking out the door.

I run back upstairs to get a sweater and to quickly change the water in Lizzy's tank. I can do this one thing. I can fix something small. I ready my room-temperature water jug and the filtering cup, and as I trace along the aquarium glass with a finger, delight sparks because my fish has finally moved. She must be better. Maybe it just took her some time to adjust. My relief builds as I search the tank for her, growing wider and hopeful, but it collapses when I find her—head down, belly up, those marvelous wispy fins stretched out on either side. I drop to my knees, both hands plastered to the tank's sides, thinking only how odd it is that Lizzy's belly is all white. I assumed it was spotted like the rest of her. I narrow my eyes on the dead fish, waiting for tears, but none come. *Crazy fucking messes* is what I think.

"I'm not sad," I say. I examine Lizzy's bloated body, whispering through clenched teeth, "My fish is dead. She's dead." I could kick myself. I've wasted my summer on a stupid fish. But no more. I race downstairs and with furious hands, I grab my tennis shoes from beside the door and stuff my feet into them, hearing again the sound that rose up from my dad's body as he threw the plants against the garage. It fills me, too. The house is so quiet now but still vibrating; I hold myself very still and hear the sound of water dripping in the sink, the rasp of car wheels on the pavement outside. I focus. I rustle for my house key in the drawer by the back door. But then comes the sound of the toilet flushing and the sink running in the downstairs bathroom. The door opens and there she is.

She walks out of the bathroom and I say, "My fish died," like it's all her fault, like she owes me an apology.

But she doesn't ask me what happened. She doesn't argue with my tone of voice. She doesn't even seem to see me.

"I know they've done it, I know they're out there. They tricked me into buying the wrong seeds."

She is covered in mud, both her arms, her knees, even her hair has mud in it. Her fingernails are thick dark crescents. There are petals and plant leaves stuck to her t-shirt. Three tomato seeds on her cheek. Her face is tense, focused inward.

"What are you talking about?" I say. My voice is hard.

She cocks her head at me. Sees me. Then her eyes narrow, "Follow me, I don't want you going out there right now."

"I'm going to Sonja's …"

"Not right now you're not."

My rebellion is to wait a moment. I don't follow her right away. But she repeats herself, "I said I don't want you out there. I want you to stay with me."

We walk in a line up the stairs and I hold tight to my little ball of fury. Leaves drop from her shoulder onto the carpet and I step on them. She goes into the bathroom, leans over the sink and turns on the water. "I've got most of them out. I'll finish it after a break." She immerses both her arms up to the elbows in the porcelain bowl. I stand behind her at the doorway. I watch her cleaning her arms so gently, so carefully.

"I said that my fish died."

She just keeps passing her forearms under the stream of water.

"Don't you even hear me?" I've raised my voice. "My fish. The one I found with George. My project. Don't you even care?"

She nods over the sink. "I hear you, but I'm telling you I've got a few more of those seeds to get out of the ground and then I'll have fixed it." She wipes the mud off her knuckles.

"What seeds? What are you talking about?"

She keeps washing her arms, running a hand up one arm and down the other. The dirt sluices off her skin and creates a dirty lake inside the wash basin. "It's a very good thing I figured this out," she says.

"Why?" There is poison in my voice and I both want her to hear it and am terrified that she'll hear it. "You're talking about seeds and I'm telling you my fish died."

"They've got a scheme going at Sky Nursery. A dangerous and deadly scheme. They've fooled everyone." Here she laughs. "And I told your father but he's just as trusting as everyone else at this point."

When she looks at me this time, her eyes are hooded and dark. She's looking at me, but I'm not anywhere in that look. I can't find myself in the face she's using to stare at me. This is not my mother.

"No. He's. Not." I say, alive now. Electric now.

"He's not what?"

"There's nothing wrong with trusting."

She moves back from the sink and is drying her arms. "What are you saying to me, Ella Tomlinson?"

I don't know what I'm saying—my body is red hot, my hands and feet filled with energy and courage—but I say it anyway, "You're wrong."

"What?"

"You're wrong. You don't know anything."

Her face grows very still. "I won't have that, Ella. You're going to behave. That is the first rule. No matter what your father says."

"You don't make the rules," I yell. "You just make stuff up!" Then I turn, ready to race down the stairs and out the door to Sonja's.

But she is behind me in a second, grabbing my elbow in the doorway.

"Get off me!" I scream.

Her hand tightens. "You're out of control, you're being unsafe!"

"You're hurting me, let me go!"

We tussle. Me pulling away and her hand like a vise on my arm. "Stop moving," she says.

I don't stop. I am fighting her with everything I've got. "You're hurting me."

"Stay still. I would never hurt you!"

My tiny body explodes with rage at this lie. She is someone who cannot, absolutely and never again, be trusted to tell me the truth. I am louder, sharper, more dangerous than I have ever felt and I shout in her face, "Get away from me, you fucking crazy mess!"

She jerks back, shocked at what I've said and I am suddenly fast as a swordfish, slick and swift with power. I slip my arm away from her before she even knows it and I strike out with the same speed. I slap her in the face and the sound is thick, sickening, as it echoes in the tiled room. Then I push against her hips and when she stumbles backward, I slam the bathroom door, putting it between us, scared of myself and of her. I kick the door hard, screaming that I hate her and I want her to leave us alone, to go far far away. But I mean me, now, too.

In five quick steps I am safe inside my bedroom and plunging a small hand into Lizzy's tank, wrapping my fingers around the slippery creature and feeling the flimsy bones break as I clench her body and race downstairs. I am outside in a flash and into the wreck of our garden. With my free hand I carve out a small hole near an upturned paper flag that reads *acorn squash* in my mother's once-tidy writing. I hurl Lizzy in and hurriedly cover the corpse with more wet mud.

The rain is falling hard as I stand up. Rain soaks the front and back of my sweater and slides onto my nose and I know that I cannot go to Sonja's. I head in the direction of George's house. But I get within a block and turn down another street. And I keep going. I zigzag, left on 60th and right on 24th, left on 59th and right on 22nd, and so on, until I hit Market street and turn around. Just walking. Keeping myself in motion. Kids are outside on their bikes even in the rain. Cars pass with their windshield wipers screeching. I walk for over an hour. Maybe even two. Before I realize it, my zigzagging brings me back to my own street. And this is when I see that the front door is wide open.

I walk up the steps. I am only ten years old. I've exhausted my anger in all my walking and all I've got left is my child's fear. The house is very quiet but I wait for a moment just inside the door. Everything is silent. I stand at the bottom of the stairs and then tiptoe up them. Listening. All of the doors upstairs are open. Not a sound comes from any of them. My room hums with the buzz from the light in Lizzy's empty tank. I step past my door toward my parent's room. Listening, both hoping and not hoping.

I don't call her name. Signs of a departure are everywhere. "She's always leaving," I sass into the still air, but it's only a whisper. "A normal parent would leave a note."

An empty duffel bag lies several feet from the closet. Two dresser drawers are slightly open, some drawers empty and some drawers draped in clothes spilling over the edges like cloth vines. Shoes litter the floor and one of my mother's winter coats is arms-wide spread across the bed. There is a gaping hole in the closet where her hanging clothes usually hang. She's left before but she's never taken anything with her.

I understand in the way you experience the pain from a burn. There's the initial contact, and at first nothing, but then it blazes and throbs. I understand her leaving is my fault. I told her to go.

I hurry back to my own room, get my savings wallet and a coat and run outside. I don't call my dad. This is my fault, and if I can just get to her in time, I can fix it. I sprint to the bus stop a few blocks away and watch the mud on my shoes dry as I ride all the way downtown. Then I get off at the pier as I've done many times before, just never alone.

It's not a problem to find the terminal, to know which doors to go in. Will she already be inside, waiting for the next ferry? Am I too late? I try to rush but I'm blocked by a large family, the kids juggling with backpacks, the parents rolling a suitcase each. Finally inside, the main terminal waiting hall is crowded with people sitting in straight rows of linked plastic seats or milling about the vending machines and coffee counter. I sweep the room, searching for her. Nothing. I check the bathrooms, the telephone cabins, the groups of people staring at the time boards. But she isn't there. It's nearly two o'clock. My dad will be off his boat and heading home already.

I am determined. I am fierce. I stand in that main hall and I weigh my options. I can give up and go home or I can get on the next boat and follow her where she must be going. My dad went to find her in Bellingham the last time, where the Skagway boat brought her back. I will do the same. I have my pass. I can still catch her. But none of the schedule boards list Bellingham. I stand below them and read them all again. None of it makes sense.

I have to think. I have to figure this out. I stand rigid, checking the schedule. She takes boats. The times she left us this summer she took a boat, didn't she? I just have to get on one. I can be brave. I think how relieved my dad will be when my mother and I will come back home together tonight. So I dare the counter, waiting what seems like ages for the line to grow shorter. I ask the woman in the Washington State Ferries uniform about the Skagway Ferry. I say this like I know what it is.

She frowns and says, "I don't know what you're talking about, young lady."

"The Alaska boats," I say, growing quieter.

She shakes her head.

"Or Bellingham?" I asked.

"We got boats to Bainbridge Island and Bremerton. That's all. If you go next door there's the boat for Canada. But that's an expensive one." She gives me a sideways glance. "You're not on your own are you?"

I shake my head, point across the room and say, "Just asking for my parents. We're visiting the city."

A man comes from behind her and says, "Yes, yes, the Alaska Service. You got to get to Bellingham to use that one. But that's a three day boat ride, how long you folks visiting?"

I shrug and smile and slink away. Then I circle the inside of the terminal, once, twice, three times. Hoping. Thinking. I know the ferries but I don't know this. She isn't here. How will I get to Bellingham? Where is Bellingham? Three days!

Groups of people are staggered about the room, everyone shuffling luggage back and forth. At the main doors, I peer outside. I walk back and forth in front of the building. There are taxis lined up and a few people waiting for them. There are several other cars whisking into the pickup/drop off space then speeding away once they've collected the person they've come for.

I pause. I walk to the end of the street. I walk back, cross the front of the terminal building and keep going on to the next corner. I will try these first streets. Walk them carefully. I have to find her. I will find her.

"Looking for someone?"

The voice comes from behind me. I turn around.

And I jump. The man only has one leg. He's holding an empty white box in one hand and a pair of crutches in the other. "It's okay," I say, backing away. "I'm meeting my mom."

"So you're going somewhere with your mom?" He has a full beard and a baseball cap. His face is tan. His lips are dry.

I shake my head, walk toward the terminal building.

He's hopping beside me, staring at me. "It was just a question, I'm just curious. I like talking to people."

I keep walking but he stays with me; he's really fast on his one leg. "Where's your mom then?"

"She's just there," I say, pointing, trying to walk even faster.

"I don't see her. Is she that blonde lady?"

I keep going. I don't answer him.

"Wait," he says, putting a hand on my shoulder. "I said, is she that blonde lady?"

I try to shake his hand off, but his fingers hold tight. "Let's go talk to her. She looks nice."

I pull again but cannot get out of his grip. I'm looking all around and there's no one paying any attention. There's no policeman. No other adults even noticing what's happening. A group of people down the street are laughing, families going about their family stuff. I start to cry and the man lets go. "Whoa! That's ok. You're okay." He puts his hand back. "Just help me along."

But I hurtle myself away from him and his hand drops. I break into a run.

"Aw now," he yells after me. "Just give a one-legged man some help!"

But he doesn't follow me and I make it to the terminal doors, run across the terminal hall to the telephone cabins. I'm crying when I get inside that cabin door and grab the receiver. The man hasn't followed me. I'm still crying but I know what to do. The telephone is sticky in my hands. I dial the operator and explain, how I've been taught at school, that I want to make a collect call.

While it rings, my breath comes in hard, sharp gasps. A few chairs away from the phone is a family of four, sitting in a row in those hard plastic seats. Father, child, child, mother. Both children—a little boy and a little girl—are drinking from a small juice box.

"Dad?" I say when he picks up.

"Oh my God, Ella, where are you?" I hear the rustling of a coat, the phone knocking against his jaw. "I've been frantic, you never called me this morning and no one's here."

"I'm downtown," I whisper to my dad.

I want to ask him if we can drive around the city together, searching for her. I want to know if he thinks we can find her like that. But instead, I just stare at the family of four and at those kids sipping on their juice boxes. The boy has a Frisbee sticking out of his backpack and is reading a comic book, he elbows his sister and shows her a page which must be funny because the girl tips her head all the way back and laughs.

Then she gets out of her seat and wriggles up onto her mother's lap to better see what her brother is reading. The mother accepts her without comment, shifting her paperback further out of the way. With a free hand she smoothes the girl's hair down.

"I'm downtown, I couldn't find her," I say. And I look down at my own hands. My fingernails are black moon crescents of dirt from our garden.

"I'm coming," he says. "I'll be there right away."

And he is. He comes running into the terminal building twenty minutes later and he finds me sitting in my chair near the phones. We leave together, just the two of us.

In the car he says, "Listen, when school starts you can take the bus, you're old enough now, and meet me at the Pier for my last two runs. Or you can go straight to George's or over to Sonja's."

"We'll figure it out," he says.

He holds his hand up for me like we should give each other a high five. But when I reach out to put my hand against his, he pulls me close and hugs me instead. Right there in the cab of his pick-up truck. Tight. I can feel him shake, can feel his heart hammering away underneath the immaculately white shirt of his ferry captain's uniform. I squeeze him back, crushing my arms together until my shoulders hurt. He doesn't mention my mother, or how I tried to find her. How I failed. So I understand right away that this time isn't like the others. I understand that we're on our own finally and my mother isn't ever coming back.

17

THERE IS ALWAYS A NO-GO ZONE, AND A WAY around it. This is what my dad taught me when we worked the different points of sail. He told me there was something useful in every angle—it all depended on the destination and the sailor's impatience. So I know that I could attempt it. I would just have to work to windward, find Neil somewhere in the house and start the whole explanation with a single word.

"Footprints," I could say.

His joy would ignite but I would just need to keep as close to the wind, keep us outside the no-go zone. He's been hoping for this, optimistic against my warnings of difficulty. I could watch his joy course through him, get his arms and hands moving, set his face alight. And I might wonder—for those few moments—if the strength of his feeling might push us further to a reach, which is the fastest way to cut through the water on most boats. But no, because this boat can't handle the speed.

So after footprints, I would pass him other words. There was never a reason to, so I haven't told him about the countries of Before and After. I haven't told him how my dad and I sailed from one to the other on a boat of our own design, how we left my mother at the border. There are reasons some women do not dream of children.

Neil is a biology professor and he doesn't know boating but he does know genetics. He does this game with his students, asking them to flip a coin 46 times. Each side of the coin is labeled Mom or Dad, and the students record their results about the probability of inheriting a gene from one parent or another. He tells them it is even more complicated than this, but this will give them some idea. The students like flipping the coins, like thinking of their chances to have inherited Dad's beaked nose or Mom's olive skin. Often a student will ask about personality traits instead of physical traits and he will launch into a discussion of how much research goes on in this area. What is nature and what is nurture? Inevitably, the students will ask about diseases. How do we know we're going to have cancer? How do we know we're going to have Parkinson's?

It's a useful game, but this boat is already beating its way across this ocean and there isn't much time. It's running a close-haul because this is the simplest navigational technique for these waters. "Guess what?" I would say. And he would turn to me, he would listen to my unsettling news. I would be able to tell him that until the photographs flew from my dad's wallet out onto the pavement and eventually made their way into my hands, the shipwreck of my mother had been buried at the bottom of the sea for so many years that I'd finally felt safe enough to consider having children. That word "until" is the one he needs to understand, the one whose letters can be arranged and re-arranged as often as you like, they will never spell "footprints."

"It's the genetics of it," I would say.

"You mean you think it's impossible?"

"No, I mean I think it's far too possible."

It would take him a moment but then: "I see." Because he'd have to.

"But that's not all."

"So tell me."

In this way, Neil would hear me confess that what terrifies me the most is that I don't know how thin these boundaries are supposed to be. I don't know the strength of the genetics and if one day I might end up creating my own countries of Before and After.

When the wind is right this would not be so difficult to say. I would say it. He would hear it. The boat would sail on. And then, "So let's not be silly and romantic about this, okay?"

"Of course not," he would assure me.

"I never should have agreed in the first place."

"I understand."

"I'm so so sorry."

"I'll go with you."

And so on and so forth until all our worries and guilt would be smoothed away. Until our decision would seem as grand and clean as a full white sail, filled with its wind, pulling our boat forward on its course.

18

THE NEXT MORNING I FIND NEIL TALKING to the dogs in the kitchen. At least I think that's what he's doing—talking to Daisie while she sits at his feet wagging her tail, but he stops when I come in. He swallows his last word.

I sit on a kitchen chair and Trapp comes to push his head against me, rest his chin on my thigh. I rub his eyebrows. I press against his warm fur.

"I'm guessing the *Ginz* has gas?" Neil says.

But I've found a scratch on Trapp's ear. I worry at it, feel along its ridge. Try to determine if it's deep. He must have cut himself out at the lake. Or running behind the bushes at the far corner of the back yard, his head down, sniffing at the earth.

"He's been out on it, don't you think? Even this winter?"

I nod, still rubbing Trapp's ear. My dad loves January Blackmouth fishing. He loves this. If he were in this room, he'd be telling us about his best spot, his best tackle. He'd be telling us how many he's already caught and that he can't wait to get back out there.

"Ella?"

I shake my head. I do not say, *we are not going.* I do not say, *how can you ask me this?* I think about those Blackmouth and my dad's happy grin when he's caught a 28-incher, and my anger rises into a sharp peak, throbbing up from my nauseous belly and radiating around my body. Such fantastic heat. My muscles are tight with it, my back straight, and for the first time in days I feel a wonderful energy.

I whip my cell phone from my pocket and call George, "You've been there, right?"

It takes him a moment but he catches up. I know vaguely that Hat Island is off the coast of Whidbey, but I don't know exactly how to get there. George tells me how, and he tells me where the rough water is, where the dangers are.

"I need to know when he told you," I say.

There's a pause. "I don't even remember, Ella. It didn't seem like a big deal at the time. Maybe a year ago. Right after he bought it. Honestly. I don't understand any of this."

I think I'm going to ask him if he wants to come with us, but those aren't the words that come out of my mouth. "If he told you a year ago, he didn't tell you right after he bought it. Do you want to know how long he's had it?"

There is another pause. Now I'm talking about their friendship.

I say it without waiting for his answer, "Six years."

George whistles low, breathes through his nose.

I see the frown on his brow. See Lisa hovering behind him, wondering what I'm saying, why George's face has gone so sour. And why does it feel so good to know that I've done this? It shouldn't, but it does.

He says, "What about your mom, Ella?"

I tell him that I'll call him later, put the phone in my pocket, turn to Neil, and say, "What are we waiting for?" because I can't answer George's question if I don't see this cabin. "It isn't George's fault and it isn't my fault, you know."

But I'm already out the door. We load the dogs into the truck and drive to the marina through a dense fog. We speak in the truck but none of it matters. We discuss how long it will take us, whether we need to be careful of the weather. I focus on the hard edge of my anger and enjoy the fire in it. When a station wagon pulls up beside us and two small dogs in the back window start to bark at our dogs, baring their teeth and scrambling at the glass, I think, yes, lunge farther, bark louder.

"Ella?"

I relax my hands in my lap and I say, "I'll drive the boat. You'll need to keep Trapp calm."

The *Ella Ginz* is a small center console, an easy ocean fishing boat for which my dad spent years saving up. At the sight of her my belly flips from rage to sorrow—quiet hours, watching my dad at the wheel—but I think of where she will take us and it flips right back. I breathe in a salty lungful of fury. I think, lunge farther, bark louder. Neil takes the dogs into the front seats. I motor the boat out of our slip and out of the harbor. Daisie is comfortable on the Sound, excited, moving between us or standing in front of the small wheelhouse like a mascot, her body rigid in the breeze. Trapp has never loved the ocean; he's only been out a few times since we rescued him. He keeps his body in contact with Neil's leg and barks when we hit the wake from a passing trawler.

We're well beyond the marina in a few short minutes, out into the open water, with the mountains looming against the gray sky. There is a strong mist today that feels almost like rain. It will soak into our jackets, soak into our jeans, into the dogs' fur, and later tonight we will all smell of the sea. We will smell like my dad after a day of ferrying or fishing. At work, my dad always took a turn on the deck or opened his window in the wheelhouse. At play, my dad could sit for hours in his quietly bobbing boat, waiting for the perfect Halibut or Rockfish. He was the smell of the sea and in my anger I want to be this, too. I want to think about the truth of him for these hard, bright minutes. Out here on the water. I know this water. I know this sky and this ocean, and this boat, and I know myself. I know my dad.

Because this is what happened—I had a mother, I had a dad. The three of us lived together in a small wooden house. This was a country named Before, which was a silly, even a fantastic place. But that didn't last. Silly turned to strange turned to scary. Then my mother left. And so my dad and I moved to a country named After. She was no longer there. Eventually we forgot about her.

A slight gap has opened up in the clouds. A hint of blue sky. A patch of water glints as we race across it, blinding me for a moment. I hold the *Ginz* steady as it leaps and crests the waves. I am going a little bit too fast but the speed feels just right, the hum of the engine working my shoulders and the way I have to hold myself firm not to be unsettled. Trapp and Neil and Daisie keep themselves low to the sides of the boat, unmoving, facing forward.

No, I think, this is not what happened. Somehow those two countries blurred in a way that I do not understand, that I was not allowed to see. I stretch my mind backward, trying to gather up the facts but the facts have slipped from my fingers and fallen into the water. I'd have to dive deep to find them and this water is too murky for that. No one opens their eyes in this water. It would sting.

The shoreline of Hat approaches, with its gray rocks and sandy ridges. Several small coves stretch east along the coast. The forest beyond these coves is a vibrant green whose upper limit is broken only by one massive rock. The peak of the rock juts above the tree line like a raised finger. A warning or a plea for silence. Without even bothering to check whether Neil can see me, I lean over the edge of the boat and vomit into the ocean. Nothing but crackers and tea, it comes quickly. I wipe my mouth on my windbreaker. Breathe. Take in more anger with the smell of the water and the salt and the seaweed.

I maneuver the *Ginz* into Hat's tiny marina, wind around to slip 82. My dad's name will be next to the slip tag and this gives me another little jolt. John Tomlinson. Written out for anyone to see like this isn't a secret. The slap of this gets me moving quickly. We dock and tie, jump out and log our arrival on the marina clipboard. The dogs leap happily around the dock while I scan the clipboard for my dad's handwriting. There is nothing on the first page but on the second I find it. John Tomlinson. Just over a week before. I throw the clipboard back onto its hook.

Neil catches up to me, "I checked a map. It will be just over there." He points away from the marina to the northwestern tip of the island. "Number 15."

"George said he had the old anchor chain from The *Kalakala*. That's how we'll know," I say.

I crackle as I walk. Electric. I am taller, and faster, and stronger. We find a trail that heads off across the beach toward a row of cabins. My shoes fill with sand but I don't care, nothing can slow me down. Neil keeps track of the dogs, leashing them at the sight of two other walkers. It's a cold day, the wind is high. My hair is whipped across my face and I have to pull a strand that has gotten stuck in the corner of my eye. It slices on the way out and I blink against sudden tears.

It's just there. A small cabin with weathered gray wood paneling. The window sills, door and porch trim are white. And I see the old anchor chain.

"That must be it." Neil reaches for my arm but I'm already moving. Terrified but moving. The beach today is stark but breathtaking. Pine trees and overgrown rhododendrons, a line of stones near the waterline, the whole thing with a view upon the Saratoga Passage. If I squint I can see the dark line of the much larger Whidbey Island to the west. Beyond the last cabin—his cabin, I force myself to think—is nothing but empty beach. We let the dogs go and they race each other up a small hillside, Daisie leading the way.

The windows are dark and while Neil fumbles in his pocket for my dad's key ring, I wait for one of them to brighten. What would I do? Would I run away? George said no one lives here, but what does George know? Neil tries all the keys and on one of them, the lock turns easily.

"Ok?" Neil says.

We step inside. I close my eyes while Neil calls out, but I can tell immediately the place is empty. The silence of it. The damp and the dark. No one could be here. Relief rushes over the sick feeling in my stomach. But this relief settles fast, turning back to anger. Okay, this place really exists but what the hell is this place? The dogs scurry about while I begin a kind of halting tour. Neil keeps behind me. The cabin is all wooden floors with muted blue carpets; the air is cold, humid. There is a small front room with a sofa and a low table. One armchair. To one side is a door that leads to a kitchen. To the other is a door to a small bedroom and bathroom. I pace the length of the front room, turn around in the tiny kitchen, open the door to the little bedroom. I pace and pace, walking faster and touching objects as I pass with my angry, trembling fingers. I knock over a vase, right it too hard and have to set it straight all over again.

"Ella?"

I don't answer him. I just keep walking around.

Sparsely furnished but clean, this place is exactly what I would expect a cabin belonging to my dad to look like. But the more I look around, the more it feels as though I have been here before and just can't remember.

Along the window sills are shells I collected with my dad as a child, and on the table water polished stones in a jar that once belonged to me. Photographs of me, and of me and Neil, rest along the small mantle above the fireplace. Several books line a small bookshelf; many are ones I gave him as gifts. Neil's gifts are here, too. Bits of forest treasure he has passed to my dad over the years. None of it makes sense. I swallow through another roll of nausea, grab a cracker packet from my pocket and tear into it.

"Ella?" Neil's eyebrows are knitted closely.

I say nothing, just eat my cracker. Then I go to the kitchen, find a glass, open the fridge and pour myself some water from one of the plastic bottles I knew I'd find there. A 12-pack from Costco. What he takes on his boat, what he keeps in his garage.

I am throwing up the water and cracker before I can stop myself. Neil is instantly behind me, rubbing my back.

"Let's sit down. Or do you just want to go? And you're getting sick."

I stand up straight, making him drop his hand. "No, I'm not." I wipe my mouth and my hands are not shaking anymore. I'm empty now. I turn and walk back into the living room, thinking of the deed, the logic somewhere. My mother has been here. Why else wouldn't my dad have told me? That injured woman he saved—with her limp or her wheelchair, or however it was she healed after her accident—she's been in this room before, I'm sure of it, and I haven't. And Cap'n Johnny has some fucking explaining to do. I open each drawer, check along each shelf, behind each book and photo, in each corner, under the sofa cushions. In my furiousness I have gotten the dogs excited and they race about, jumping up onto the couch and back down again. Daisie knocks

Trapp into a wooden chest near the front window. I hadn't realized it was a chest, that it might be something else I could open. I kneel down. Tilt. Breathe. Tilt. I remember this chest. I don't remember when it was no longer in my dad's bedroom.

I open it. At first it looks like the chest is filled with cardboard. That's all. Pieces of cardboard. But when my eyes adjust to the symmetry, I see it is really filled with boxes. Plain cardboard boxes stacked alongside one another. Not exactly the same size, but close. I lift one and place it on the floor. Lift out another. And then another. They're labeled. Each one has a number on it. I pick up number 17 and open it to see a jumble of items: a small flashlight, a white linen sachet tied with a string, an empty jam jar, a pencil sharpener. The sachet smells of cinnamon, cloves, cardamom. I pass the box to Neil. In Number 4 there are a series of hollowed out gourds in the shape of utensils: a ladle, a shallow spoon, a serving fork, thick, flat chopsticks, another spoon. None of these are things my dad would have purchased. More like Lisa's style, but she would know better than to give them to my dad. In this same box is a hardbound book titled *The Eagle*, but when I open the pages it turns out to be a book safe with a secret compartment. My hands are shaking now, but I keep opening them. In Number 7 are three empty jam jars and several carved wooden figurines—a whale, an osprey, a salmon. They are intricate and stunning. I put the whale in my pocket. This box also contains a knitted hat—gray with a stripe of navy, and then a scarf, this time lilac, with thin threads of heather. This scarf is feminine and soft but it's the colors that stop me first.

Here she walks into a fabric store, she's holding my small hand and with the other she gestures to the bolts of fabric lining the walls. We find the purples and we stand there ticking them off from lavender to plum and everything in between. "Redheads and purple," she says with a wink. "It's a color that makes us even taller, even better."

So here she walks into this room, into this cabin. And I know that all of these objects have some connection to her. I open more boxes and find more items: beeswax candles, a pencil carved from a tree branch and a pressed-flower paper notebook, a pair of knitted gloves.

Neil is behind me. "What is all that?"

My hands are shaking as I take out each and every box. There are thirty-six of them. All labeled. Underneath these boxes are a small stack of documents. Papers. Letters. Some in rubber bands, some just free. I don't want to read them, don't want to see her scrawling handwriting again, but when I get brave enough to look I see that the cards bear my father's name but are unsigned. I don't recognize the handwriting. And the papers are from someone named Reza. Erica Reza, with a Portland, Oregon address. I rock back on my heels and read them. The dogs have quieted now, and I move between them on the rope rug, leaning against the couch and using their bodies to warm me. I have grown terribly cold in this room. No, these letters are not from my mother but it only takes me a moment to determine that they are about my mother. The tone is informative, kind, but not overly friendly. They are essentially progress reports. I skim them, learning that she is walking better, she is interacting with house members, she is taking her meals with the community. Inside two of the envelopes is a business card for Erica Reza, MSW. I pocket them both, put the letters back in the chest.

I've emptied the contents of the chest onto the carpet so I put everything back in again. Neil is looking at me, but I don't want his looking.

"When was the last time you saw her?" Neil asks.

"She left when I was ten."

"I know that," he says. His voice is exasperated. "But you never saw her after that?"

"Never," I say. "I've told you this. She was gone. He never found her."

Neil shakes his head, says in a quiet, quiet voice, "Except it seems that he did."

A current moves through me from toe to face.

Neil is staring out the window now. Thoughtful. "Maybe she can explain everything, maybe she's had help."

This idea breaks what is left of my kindness. "Then I should be rejoicing shouldn't I? What luck to lose one parent and have another just waiting in the wings!"

He frowns and I can see him preparing my dad's defense.

"I know, I know," I snap, gesturing to the room and what it implies, "he's never lied to me, right?"

"Ah, Ella, that would be so much easier, wouldn't it? If you could just fight your way through this."

A kind of sharp pleasure ignites. I can make him angry, too.

"I know," he says, his voice cracking, "let's go yell at your dad. That should help."

I kneel down, gather the items from the chest all over again. I throw the gourd utensils against the far wall, rip that potpourri sachet and let the spices fly. The dogs chase them, Daisie yips with delight.

Neil silences her with a stern "No."

Then to me, "Oh, God, Ella – we have to stop this. We're exhausted. Maybe you need to lie down. You've hardly slept. We've hardly slept."

I pitch a pair of gloves at the front window. "Sure, we learn that in vet school. A good night of sleep can cure anything."

"Would you please stop?"

But I can't. I grab the scarf and race out of the cabin. The dogs follow and dart ahead. I break into a run. Hear Neil yelling. Halfway down the beach, I startle a fisherman but I race on, only a few hundred feet and I am at the water's edge and can throw the scarf into the waves. But the awful thing won't sink and I have to wade in, stomp on it, drown it. My feet are instantly cold in the icy January water, but I stay where I am, and I twist the scarf with my fingers until the wool is finally saturated and gets taken away with the undertow.

Neil catches up and shouts, red-faced now, "Stop escaping! It isn't fair. It never is."

I am thrilled by his anger. It is not easy to make Neil lose his temper but now I am set on fireworks.

I start walking down the beach, back toward the marina. My teeth clack, my heavy wet jeans slow me down.

"Don't do this! Not now!"

He catches up again and for the first time in our relationship, he puts a hand on my arm and he yells in my face. "Stop running away! Stop doing this!" But he isn't angry enough, he calms down too quickly. "I know you're not really angry with me. Please!"

But whatever he wants from me, I can't take it. I turn away again and keep walking. Knowing my refusal to meet him in this conversation can only make him angrier. I need the explosion. I want the bright lights and smell of smoke. I hunker into the wind, my shoulders closed, my legs moving fast. I am waiting for another shout, waiting for him to push me, grab me, or kick at the sand. My thigh muscles burn from walking so fast. The back of my throat stings from my ragged breathing.

But he keeps pace with me, and the voice which reaches me is quiet. Sympathetic. Enraging. "We'll find her together. I'll help you. You are not alone in this, Ella."

I half-turn toward him, I spit out the words. "I'm so not alone, I'm even pregnant."

Telling him is so selfish. I say it to prove my own victimhood, to wrap myself up in the suffocating blanket of my dad's death, to barricade my mother in her far away country. He has no right to think that I might want to see her again and to prove this, I give him the biggest reason.

This time he stops me, yanks so hard on my arm that we both stagger. Face each other with the wind at our throats. The dogs are yipping around us. He makes me repeat my phrase.

I watch his face evolve again, first shock, then tentative joy, then confusion. Finally, a pinched misgiving.

"How pregnant are you?"

I wait a moment. Then hazard the truth. "Not very. A few weeks."

He is holding himself very tight, watching me. Wounded animals are either helpless or dangerous. It is difficult at first to tell which. "Why are you only telling me now?"

I study his face. His light eyes and hair. The thin scar above his eyebrow. The hollow at the base of his throat. I wait, silent, hoarding him into myself. Knowing that this will be an ending of sorts, that I can build a wall. That I must. Me building it from these images of him. Making this distance between us.

"Because this is the only time we're ever going to talk of this."

Neil looks away from me. Moves his eyes off of me and onto his own hands and keeps them focused there. On himself. He does not look back at me. I take a breath. I feel him draw further and further away. There is a relief in this. A pressure removed. How easy it is to destroy Neil's unmarred history. With just a handful of words I've created his first real catastrophe. Made him just a little bit more like me.

19

So maybe the call came when I was at track practice. This would have been a bit of luck. The phone ringing in the late afternoon, my dad home before his once a week late night run to Bremerton. Maybe the phone rang at the exact moment that Cassandra Weltman nudged past me to win the 200M dash. Maybe while I stood, thighs burning and with my head tipped back to get more air, my father was causally picking up the receiver of the telephone at our house.

Of course my dad never casually picked up that phone because he would have known what kind of news could be waiting—that they'd found her body, or parts of her body. Only enough to identify her.

"I'm looking for someone named John Tomlinson," the woman might have said.

I see him. I see him nod without speaking. I see the tension in the hand holding that phone. I see him accept the woman's introduction and her careful request that he sit down, that she has something upsetting to tell him.

He would have tested the feeling of relief—how could he not?—he would have let it rise up and sit next to him at the kitchen table. Eight years. At least he would finally know. "Go ahead."

Maybe it was a simple exchange. "We've found this woman. We

think it's your wife." And then my dad jumping out of the house, racing to his car, speeding down the highway.

But then he would have had to find a way to go south without telling me. Spend the night in Portland and not let me know. And why would he have done that? Why wouldn't he have told me about the call?

So maybe the call came while I was already away? Spending the night at a friend's house, or at a track meet across the state? However it happened, I think about the space of those few hours as he drove south, the change in him. He would have become a man who passed on the right, on the left, who flashed his lights at slow drivers and made gestures, whose foot could not seem to touch the brake but only the accelerator.

Maybe she would have still been in surgery when he arrived. Maybe he even had to wait for her to wake up. But when she did, when he could go in to see her, what would it have been like for him to see her for the first time in so many years? To see what eight years of living mostly on the streets had done to her. He wouldn't have been alone. Nurses, the surgeon, other staff members. A social worker.

Maybe she is incredibly thin. Maybe her hair is dirty, cut short and ragged. Maybe her skin is bruised and dirty. Maybe her fingernails are ragged. Has she done drugs? Are there bruises and needle tracks? Has she sold herself? Does it show? Is she missing teeth? Are they black?

Maybe she's wrapped in bandages because of her accident. Maybe they've had to shave her head. Maybe her face is bruised, maybe her wrist is broken, several fingers bloodied and raw.

My dad waiting for the moment my mother opens her eyes.

My dad checking her face, trying to find the answers to his questions in the amount of visible damage done to her body.

Maybe my dad says her name, "Maggie?"

Maybe my mother opens her eyes. Maybe she blinks, shifts, sees everyone.

"Maggie?"

She does not answer.

"Maggie? You've had an accident."

Maybe she is watching the ceiling. Maybe her body tenses and the entire room takes in a breath, because maybe she begins to scream and tear at her tubes and bandages. Scratch at her face and thrash in her bed. Because maybe everyone in the room, including my dad and the doctor and the nurses, are part of her delusion at that moment, whatever it was or whatever it had become in those eight years. So maybe she just keeps screaming and fighting, and they try really hard to stop her but they cannot. Maybe she falls into a seizure and has to be sedated. Maybe it takes a really long time for her body to settle, for her to stop hurting herself. Maybe my dad has to leave the room, speak with the social worker.

Maybe the social worker tells him that my mother is still incredibly unwell.

Maybe he cries, his body slumped against the hospital wall, his sobs shuddering through his shoulders, snot running from his nose.

Maybe they suggest she needs a lot more care. Maybe they suggest she will never be like the woman he once knew.

Maybe this is why he never says anything to me.

20

WHAT STRIKES ME FIRST IS HOW MUCH this waiting room matches my own waiting room in Wenatchee. Same black plastic chairs, same dim light, same water tower in the corner, and same coffee table with magazines and brochures. In my waiting room the brochures are about ticks and parasitic disorders of cats and animals, here the brochures are about lactation and venereal disease. But even the set-up is similar, with the nurse-receptionist tucked into the front left corner. As I hand her my filled-out information sheet, I notice that the only thing completely missing is the smell of the animals. And in Wenatchee there are no plants. Instead, here, there are ferns and orchids in a display by the window.

Ferns and orchids. I think about this, what an odd combination it is. And I see again the nurse behind her high counter with its set-in desk, and I wonder if she's the orchid lady. There is a bright magenta hair clip in her hair, the same color as one of the orchids at the window. The exact same color, so then I think that she must be the orchid lady, and I see her tending them in the evenings when the patients have all gone, talking to them, turning their pots around to catch the earliest morning sunshine the next day. I see her scowl at the ferns. Those aren't hers and she dislikes their spiky leaves, their deep green, their sprawl and those dusty spores on the undersides of the leaves. The ferns must belong to the doctor. And then I see the disputes that must arise, the doctor wanting her ferns, the receptionist wanting her orchids.

"Ferns belong outside," the nurse says.

No, this isn't what she says. She has said, "Ms. Tomlinson? You may go in now. Second door on the left."

And so I get up. As I pass her, I compliment her orchids, but she just laughs and waves her arm at the window, "Gifts from a former patient. I'm just lucky they like that spot, I've got the blackest thumb."

I have to stop halfway down the hallway to catch my breath, even lean against the wall for a moment.

"Are you alright?"

I shake my head. I'm fine. I just made a mistake is all.

"Ms. Tomlinson?" the nurse is coming toward me and I straighten up, tell her that I'm fine.

"Just a little dizzy," I say, trying to smile. I want to ask her about the ferns now too, whether they belong to the doctor, but I bite my tongue on the words. I don't know anything about these people. I don't know what made me jump to such strange conclusions.

"Come with me and sit down," she says. She takes my hand, says that I'm cold, and she leads me into the second door on the left. "You're here for a pregnancy test, yes."

I nod.

"Have you been dizzy for awhile?"

I shake my head. "Just this morning."

She looks at me carefully. "The doctor should be right in. But let's take your blood pressure first."

She helps me off with my sweater and then slides the cuff onto my arm. I'm breathing carefully. I know how to calm myself down. I think about walking along the beach with Trapp as the nurse pumps air into the cuff. Her hand on my wrist is warm and gentle. I can see myself walking in the deep sand, my shoes off, Trapp scouring for seaweed. I place one foot above the other while the cuff tightens around my wrist, while my heartbeat grows strong and then faint again.

"You're okay," she says with real relief in her voice. She smiles at me, "Scared me for a moment. You were really pale out there."

I force a smile at her. "I've just been rushing around a lot this morning. That'll teach me."

She nods, and the doctor opens the door and shuts it behind her. The nurse gives her my blood pressure numbers and then leaves. The doctor skims my file, then nods at me. It's been several years since I've seen her and she's aged. I remember that she's a no-nonsense kind of doctor. She likes facts and research.

"Good to see you," she says.

I agree, although I can tell she doesn't really remember me.

She glances at my chart, at my information sheet. "You still live in Wenatchee? Or are you back in Seattle for good."

"Just a visit."

She nods. "Date of your last period was … ?" she scans the paperwork in front of her.

"I don't know. I never really know."

She's caught up now, I can see it on her face. "You've had painful fibroids recently? Lots of bleeding?"

I shake my head. "Not for some time."

"When were you last checked?"

"My regular exam," I say, counting, "My regular exam last summer. I had two small ones, but they didn't bother me."

"And you've been trying to get pregnant?"

She has turned back to her paperwork, so I can shake my head and say "yes" at the same time. I say this very quietly.

She looks up from the chart. "Well," she smiles. "It seems you've maybe outsmarted those troublesome fibroids. Let's do a blood test."

The blood test takes only a few moments. I watch my blood pump into the little vial. The nurse comes in with a glass of water.

"Don't want you getting dizzy again."

The doctor says she'll call me later that afternoon to confirm the results, and then she walks away, her feet shuffling on the carpeted hallway.

I say thank you. I wait a moment in my seat. But then I cannot wait any longer. I walk back down the hallway, ignoring the startled glances from the other two women in the waiting room, ignoring the nurse who looks up in alarm as I pass.

I knock, briefly, on the door I've seen the doctor go into. It's her office. She is there behind a desk, typing something into a computer. It's about me, I'm sure. She's entering her notes from the appointment, she's this kind of conscientious doctor.

"You must know," I say. "I won't keep it."

She keeps very still. She does not react. So much so that I'm not sure she's understood me. The nurse is behind me now, saying, "You can't just walk back here."

But the doctor must have understood me because she says, "It's okay, Alice. Come in, Ella."

So I sit on the chair in front of her desk and I say it again, "I won't be able to keep … if I'm pregnant, I mean. Which I'm sure I am. Urine tests are rarely wrong, the blood test will confirm it."

"We'll know for sure in a few hours."

"That's fine," I say, surprised at how firm my voice is. "But when we get that confirmation, I won't be keeping it."

She is silent. Watching me for a moment. Her office is small but lined with shelves and its shelves are filled with books and three-ring binders, all of them labeled very carefully. On each shelf sits a fern in a small pot. On each shelf the triangular leaves spill out across the book spines and binder columns.

"So the ferns are yours," I say.

She furrows her brow. "What you're saying is that you'd like to interrupt this pregnancy, if we confirm that you're pregnant?"

I nod. I look her in the eye. Then, "They're lovely. My husband would enjoy talking to you about them."

She tips her head at me. "I do love ferns."

There is a moment of silence. We stare at one another. Then she says, "I'll call you this afternoon when we get the results. I'll want to speak with you more at that time."

"Of course," I say.

"And you need to know that we don't perform voluntary interruptions here in this office."

"You don't?"

She shakes her head. "It's easier to leave this to the clinics. But I can refer you, if you're sure." She looks about to say something else, then stops.

"You don't think it's odd, mixing orchids with ferns?" I ask before I can stop myself. My hands are shaking. I hear the crazy in my voice.

There is a short pause, and then, "I think it's an odd combination, yes. But it's turned out rather lovely."

"Thank you," I say.

"You're welcome," she says.

21

"I'm going to start going through the basement." This is how Neil breaks our silence the next day, coming into the living room where I'm drinking tea and sorting the mail.

"The man from the insurance is going to call again," I answer. I do not say, my doctor confirmed my pregnancy yesterday afternoon while you were out walking the dogs.

"Well, you know everything," he says. The line of his jaw is tight, furious.

"I think so," I say. I also do not say that she gave me the name of a clinic in north Seattle.

He stands in the doorway.

He stands in the doorway and I do not tell him that I called and made a first appointment.

In his hands is a paper bag from the bakery up the street. He folds it in half, then in quarters. He stands in the doorway, keeps folding the paper bag. "You should talk to him," he says. The bag is now an eighth of its usual size, then a sixteenth, and Neil is pressing along an edge, trying to force a straight crease. I watch his hands, watch them working over the paper. He can't seem to make it small enough and he just keeps pressing and pressing. His knuckles are white with the effort.

"I know, Neil," I say. "I know."

He drops the paper onto the table, "Are you willing to consider that you're completely wrong?"

The paper slowly unfolds from its impossible creases. I look at Neil and I might be shaking my head, I might be holding very still, but it doesn't matter because he's already sitting down next to me at the table. He takes the stack of mail from me and he pushes it onto the floor. He reaches for me with one of his strong beautiful hands and I just stand up and back away.

"Please, Ella," he says.

"We have to talk about this," he says.

Ok, I think. Sure, we have to talk about this. "Where should we start?" I say, walking over to the bookshelf. All I will have to do is take out a book and flip to the back page, and there will be notes. Dates, facts, arrows pointing from one word to another. None of it will make any sense but it will show him how she was. My dad has gotten rid of many of her books but if I test every single book on this shelf, I'm sure I'll find one.

"What are you doing?"

"I'm looking for one."

"For what?" He stands up.

"Just wait."

There on the first shelf, however, is my dad's address book. We've been looking for this; George asked us for it so he could extend all the right invitations for the memorial service. I pick it up and place it on the table, then return to the shelf and start skimming the titles. Gardening textbooks and mystery novels, my dad's collection of baseball legends. All these old paperbacks. I'm sure some of hers will still be here.

But Neil stops me by picking up the little address book and saying,

"Maybe she's in here. Maybe it's just that simple. We could see for ourselves."

He fingers the thin pages and I startle at the idea that it might be this easy. Turn a page, find a mother.

Neil says, "Maybe she's fine. Maybe it's all different than what you believe. Maybe you know nothing about it."

"Stop," I say, taking the book from him and holding it tightly closed. I'm thinking of my dad writing her name in its pages, her telephone number, like she were an ordinary person, a member of his usual circle of friends and family.

Neil has crossed his arms over his chest. He says, "You don't really look the same, you know. I thought you did. But you don't. Not at all."

I'm thinking of my dad with a pencil in his hand, copying out the letters of her name and the numbers needed to reach her. I open the book and turn the thin pages. Quickly. I find everyone I expect to find: George and Lisa, myself and Neil, my dad's neighbors and other friends, the members of his quiz team, and all the other ferry captains listed with the names of their boats—the *Salish*, the *Yakima*, the *Champoeg*, the *Sealth*. But there is nothing for Maggie Tomlinson. No "M", no nothing. She isn't there. I drop the book on the table with a small feeling of triumph.

"See?" I say.

"No, I don't see. So okay, she won't be so easy to find. But what does that mean? Aren't you even a little curious to know about them? If your mother is better? As soon as we have to deal with the estate, we'll have to anyway. If she's alive, she gets the cabin."

I interrupt him, I'm speaking slowly. "I do not want this trade. If you cannot understand that, then ..."

"Then what?"

I can't answer him.

"Not even for your dad? Don't you want to know what happened?"

"This isn't about them anymore," I say, "This is my life."

Neil is staring at me. His nostrils are flared, his hair a mess where he's ruffled it in frustration. His eyes are wide, shocked.

"She left," I say.

And I wait for a second because Neil looks down at his hands again. Is thinking of himself again, of what I told him we would never ever speak about.

"She became a different person, a crazy person, and then she left," I say. "Is that what you wanted me to say?"

"My dad and I stayed," I say.

"That's not it," he interrupts me.

"I know what happened. I know how we dealt with it. On our own. We didn't need her."

"Stop thinking you know everything. That you can control everything."

"I know we learned to live without her," I say.

Neil stands up, dismissing me. He narrows his eyes. "No. You did. We don't know yet what your dad learned."

He has backed into the kitchen and I'm up and after him, gripping his shoulder with a tight hand. But he shakes me off, stepping back, blinking at my anger. "You're being completely unreasonable."

His eyebrows come down. His lips press together. "Ella, I have torn the storage room apart, looking for an explanation. Something else. Letters, something to you. He would not have lied just to lie." He throws a hand up. "And you know this, you don't need me to tell you your dad was a good man. How much more evidence do you need before you'll see that you're getting it all wrong?" He waits for this, as if he needs to let it sink in, and then he spits the words, "Frankly, Ella, I'm disgusted at how little credit you're willing to give him."

I look away. Neil isn't really disgusted with my anger at my dad. Worried, probably. Disgusted, no. He's disgusted about us, about me. It must feel good to finally tell me this.

"I can't …"

"Yes, I know." His hands are shaking as he crosses them over his chest. "You can't. You've made that pretty clear."

I could try to find something to pull us out of our anger. A pledge. An explanation. An endearment. But I don't. My rage is so much easier to live with. It wants so much less of me.

Neil pours himself a glass of water. I watch him wrestling to keep control. How far can I push him? When he's done he rinses the glass under the tap and sets the clean glass down on the drying rack. Slowly. Too slowly. He opens a cupboard by the dishwasher and gets out Daisie and Trapp's food dishes. The two dogs materialize by his side but he drops the empty dishes onto the floor and slams the cupboard door so hard it cracks on its hinges.

But before he can yell whatever he wants to yell, I am yelling first and God it feels so good to yell, and Neil must think so too because he yells back, and before we know it, we're both just shouting and pointing our fingers, crossing our arms, tightening our bodies against the other with the assuredness of our opposing positions—

"Maybe they worked it all out!"

"You have no idea what it was like!"

"I don't care how it was! This isn't about 'was', this is about 'now'!"

But no matter how much he calls me back to the question of my pregnancy, the details of my parent's story come to rest between us like something Neil has picked up on one of his forest walks and wants to give me. Only, for the first time, he has no idea what kind of object he's discovered and I do, I've seen this thing before, and I know he should have been more careful, he should not have picked this up with his bare hands, I know it might be radioactive or poisonous. I just want him to drop this thing, bury it right back into the ground, throw it into the river.

Trapp becomes so alarmed at all this yelling that he's barking at us, and he jumps up on Neil, then down to the floor and jumps up on me in turn. I stagger backward, and he keeps barking. Neil shouts him down but he barks back at us, even baring his teeth. Trapp has never done this and it silences us. In our silence, he lies down on the floor between our feet, puts his head on his paws. I walk into the bathroom to find a tissue. When I return to the kitchen, Neil has fed the dogs and is standing with his back to me.

The dogs finish eating and Neil leans over to remove their dishes. He rinses them in the sink, dries them, and then folds the dishtowel into a neat square. I pick up the address book again and finger the gold lettering on the cover. He stacks the dog dishes on the sideboard and despite the cold weather he opens the window over the sink. A thin knife of wind cuts into the warmth of the room.

Then, without turning around, Neil says, "You know as well as I do how much your dad would have loved a grandchild."

This is true. This is so true I can no longer breathe. And for this awful moment, I am relieved that my dad has died. I am so thankful, for a few horrible seconds, that he is gone. That I won't also have to answer to him. But after this fleeting feeling comes and goes, I want only to invite an attack by a rabid dog, to be torn limb from disloyal limb by its merciful teeth.

22

THAT EVENING WE EAT SUPPER WITH George and Lisa. From the moment we arrive, everyone is pretending. I am pretending not to want to vomit at the smell of the mussels cooking in broth on the stove, pretending that my body isn't aching, my breasts swollen and painful. Neil is pretending not to ignore me. George is pretending that the sight of me doesn't make him even sadder. Only Lisa is being honest, doing what she does best and trying to smooth out all of our wrinkles. She has lit scented candles and tactfully gotten George to forgo a beer for a mug of herbal tea. She is talking to Neil about aromatherapy, asking me if I'll carry one of her healing crystals.

George and I sit on the sofa in the living room, away from Neil and Lisa in the kitchen. Their living room always smells of incense and this, unexpectedly, quiets my stomach. I cross my arms over my chest to ease the pain in my breasts.

We talk about George's work, the weather, sports. He tells me about a small dispute with a neighbor. A problem with his truck. He rubs his face. When he pulls his hands away, I notice how red his eyes are.

Finally, he picks at a thread from a throw blanket and says, "You never told me what you found at the cabin." I see the boxes and those strange items in the chest. The purple scarf. I feel my anger bubbling up again, the thought of this trade. The disorder of my mother for the quiet of my father. But that's not even right. Because the sides don't match up—my father's lies for my mother's mess? I don't want that. And George should be mad about this, too. Instead he says, "What was there? Anything?"

"Nothing too interesting." I am unable to keep my voice gentle, disinterested. "Fishing poles, dishes, some magazines and seashells."

He pulls air in through his teeth. "You were his life, Ella."

"One of them," I say. "Let's keep things straight, I was just one of his lives."

"You know that's not true. And we don't know why yet. What else did you find?"

"Provisions."

At his confused glance, I repeat, "Provisions. Which only proves that he was just as cracked as you-know-who. The place was filled with empty jam jars and cardboard boxes, if that tells you anything." And once I've gotten started, I cannot stop. I tell him about the gourd utensils and the potpourri sachets, the knitted items and the candles. "All just a bunch of useless crap. And none of it means anything, not a tiny bit. Stuff my dad wouldn't even have liked."

"I don't understand."

"Neither do I!"

"Did you bring it back?"

"Why bother?" I say, frustrated that he wants to waste energy on this. Why is everyone treating this like a worthwhile mystery? "It was all just ridiculous. Meaningless."

I'm about to go on, but he sits up and frowns at me. "That's enough, Ella. You are not the only one who lost someone this week."

My anger sharpens to a point. I resent the tone of his voice. Like he was speaking to a child. My dad never spoke to me like that. "I know," I say, snapping, but then I remember that my dad kept things from me. This appears to be the graver sin.

"You know," George continues, "I used to be jealous of your mother. She was outrageously funny, at least in the beginning. No one could get a room of people laughing as quickly as your mother could. But then she changed, and things were different. You don't expect that kind of rapid change. You can't." He rubs one hand with the other, says, "He could have simply forgotten her. Left her out there somewhere, to die maybe, and moved on."

I freeze with the thought that this is what I required of him. This is what I wanted him to do, wanted us to do.

"Didn't you ever talk about her?"

The honest answer would be that we never talked about her because she took up so much space anyway. I shake my head.

"But didn't you have questions?"

"Questions about what?" Lisa asks, bustling in from the kitchen. Neil is behind her, carrying three flat wooden boxes.

George offers me a small gift by answering Lisa with: "Nothing, honey. Don't mind us."

Lisa gives us both a look but doesn't press us. Neil and I avoid each other's eyes. Then Neil and Lisa sit down at the dining room table and Lisa pushes away a stack of papers and a vase of dried flowers.

"I found all of these with Sam," she says. "I've been meaning to show you. To you, especially," she says to Neil. It's her collection of bird feathers. Sam is her oldest grandson but still young enough to enjoy walking with his grandmother to search out and gather forest treasure.

She has them all labeled and arranged in shallow glass-covered boxes, like picture frames, each quill laid out in careful rows. Neil ticks them off: Mew Gull, Laughing Gull, Bonaparte's Gull, Franklin Gull.

There's a box for songbird feathers, too.

"They're stunning," he says. He opens the latch on one of the boxes, draws out a tiny feather. At first it is just brown and boring but he holds it to the light, points at the striping, the vivid slash of yellow.

There is another box for pigeon, and one for crow and heron and raptor.

Lisa bends over the raptor box, tells us a story about finding one of the feathers and then being surprised by the falcon. "It swooped in at us. I think it wanted its feather."

She laughs. Lisa is someone who never pretends. She fills the moment with her memory and the emotion she draws from it. She single-handedly changes the air in the room.

And so it feels almost normal when Neil picks up the heron box and says, "Remember that heron, Ella?"

I tell him that I do but as soon as our eyes meet, we both look down. We continue pretending as he tells Lisa and George about the camping trip we took when we were first dating, and the injured heron we saved. Lisa tells us how she and Sam have already saved seventeen birds together. And even an owl. That was Sam's favorite.

This bird conversation carries us through our meal and an easy dessert and then Neil and I are excusing ourselves, refusing George's offer to drive us home and walking the few blocks back to my dad's with our jackets buttoned tightly. Our hoods pulled quick to our faces against the drizzle. We are silent. No longer pretending. We don't manage a single word between us as we walk along the cold sidewalk but I am remembering that heron all over again. I am remembering how we spotted it across the marsh we'd stumbled upon, how we went closer, how shocked we were that it didn't fly away. Then we saw its leg twisted up with a piece of submerged garbage or twine, and how agitated it was at being trapped. It reared its head and spread its wings to their full six-foot extension.

"Can we try and free it?" Neil whispered.

I was not sure that we should try.

Neil unlocks the back door, ushers me inside, and I remember how still we were that day, how we tried to make whirring noises and calming clicks, but it was all useless. The heron grew more upset and pulled harder at its foot; as it thrashed and struggled a cloud of blood billowed around its foreleg.

Which is when I knew we couldn't help it. And I said as much to Neil. He wanted to try to subdue it, and I told him to give up. But he refused, shaking his head at me and focusing on the bird. I remember how he took another step toward the helpless bird. I watch him shake his head now, even if I haven't asked him a question, and then he's stepping into the bathroom and shutting the door behind him. The house is cold, but I'm taking my coat off anyway and I see the heron unfold its neck and let out a growl. It tried to lift itself again and more blood emptied into the water.

"Stop moving! You're killing it."

Neil turned to me. "We can't just leave it."

But that's exactly what I had decided to do that day. If I couldn't save it, I would get as far away from it as possible. Let nature take its course when the next hungry fox or mountain lion came near.

"Maybe it's more important for this heron to become food for another animal."

"Are you serious?"

"I'm just saying we don't have the tools to get it free without hurting it irreparably. If it breaks its leg it is as good as dead."

"If it gets eaten by a fox it is also dead."

"So you see it's already too late." I remember wanting to remind him I was about to become a vet. I had taken ethics classes, dissected and autopsied, and even learned how to put an animal to sleep. I understood humane decisions were not always easy ones. "We just have to accept some things are out of our control."

He shook his head. "I have to try."

He's out of the bathroom now, giving me a nod that I can go in and brush my teeth if I want to. But I just stare at him until he turns and walks upstairs.

What patience Neil had that day. He would take one step and wait for the bird to quiet, creeping forward only a few inches at a time. I kept my distance, a little hurt but mostly certain I was right. I was sure Neil would end up torturing the already injured bird and would have to concede he'd let his romantic notions mar his scientific reasoning.

But before he reached the heron, he took a long step and removed his coat at the same time. I knew he would try to cover the bird but I also knew he wouldn't be able to hold it and disentangle the foot by himself. And now the bird was getting wild, hopping and flapping its massive wings. Neil stilled one last time, stood frozen, but the bird did not calm down this time. So he threw his coat over the bird's head and reached around to pin its wings. But what he hadn't counted on was the utility of the bird's beak, the way it sliced right through the flimsy plastic of his windbreaker. I saw that Neil would fail. Unless I helped. I did not want Neil to fail, and so I dove for the bird's legs and plunged my hands into the mud at its feet. The flat side of its beak struck the top of my head, its growls and squawking filled the air. I was soaking wet, Neil was up to his knees in mud and pond water. But then somehow the bird was free, pushing off my back with its good foot, wings beating down on my head with a surprising gentleness. I remember how I could smell the mud on its thin legs and the dusty warmth of its long torso. We watched it float away to the far end of the marsh where it settled on a log.

I remember how Neil turned to me with a triumphant smile. An *I told you so* that burst forth like a geyser from his well of safe memories and impossible stability, from his vast reservoir of confident daring. An *I told you so* that revealed exactly how far Neil would go to correct what he considered a gross injustice.

So it should not surprise me so much that even as angry as he is, Neil is not quite ready to give up on us, on me. Before lunch the next day, he hands me two gifts: in one hand is a small branch from a cedar tree, and he gives me this without ceremony, says only, "incense-cedar, these cones are shaped like geese in flight." I take the branch and hold it; I say, "oh," and "thank you," and he reaches forward like he might take it back. His gesture sits between us—both his gift and his hesitation. Can I give him something in return? I have nothing. I stare at the pinecones, at the split where the "wings" are. Neil lets out a low whistle between his teeth, but then he's handing me something else. In his other hand is Erica Reza's business card. I step back but he holds it steady.

"I think we should try."

"What? Call her?"

"We have nothing to do until tomorrow and the service. I think we should go and see her."

It takes me two tries—my hand stretching, retreating, stretching again—but I finally take the social worker's card in my hand. *Erica Reza, MSW, 23rd Street Project, 2324 Knott St.* The other card, the pair to this one, is hidden inside my shirt, plastered across my skin below my collarbone where I have been wearing it since taking it from the cabin. This card gives me everything I need for an impersonal contact—a telephone number, an email address. I could just send her my questions and let the electricity of fiber optic cables do all the work.

Neil insists, "It isn't far. We can go and be back by tonight. Don't you want to find her first? Before a judge has to, or a lawyer? Just to know?" But he changes tactics, tries another angle, "Don't you want to know what really happened? Give your dad the benefit of the doubt?"

"This card is maybe really old."

"Nine years. I counted. The letters from her to your dad stopped nine years ago." He pauses and I don't realize how I've reacted until he says, "What? Yes, I counted. I want to understand."

He reaches a hand to his forehead, presses the skin on the bridge of his nose. He continues. "Nine years isn't that long. And it's a place. An organization. So I looked it up online to be sure. It's still there."

"You looked it up online?"

"Didn't you?"

I am still holding the card. Yes, I have already looked it up. Quietly, on my cell phone, standing alone in the house. I also know that this place still exists. And I know that it's an intermediate housing solution for people with psychological disorders, transitioning from the streets back into "normal" life.

"OK," Neil says, a sudden volume to his voice. "Ok, Ok. So John messed up. Or something else was going on. So you're angry. You've read the reports she sent."

"Only once, just to know what they were."

He holds up his hand. "Why shouldn't you read them? You should read them again and again. Wouldn't you rather know what you're dealing with than continue to fight against the fact that you were left in the dark?"

"I'm not fighting anything."

He snorts, but there is no humor in the sound. "You're furious, Ella. You're so furious you've decided to ruin everything else. Including us."

I hold the social worker's card back toward him. I know what he's saying. What he wants me to realize. "I was always ambivalent about children. One thing does not have anything to do with the other."

"I call bullshit on that."

"My appointment is already made."

Neil's jaw is tight. "When?"

"It doesn't matter," I say, dropping the card on the floor.

"Like hell it doesn't matter!" He folds his arms over his chest and stares at me. There is a challenge on his face but there is also so much fear. I've done this—I've made him fearful. "You can't not tell me. You can't be that insane."

Eye to eye for an instant. Does he mean this? Will he take those words back? But he says nothing. And all I say is that my appointment is for the day after the memorial service. I don't tell him it's a first appointment. I don't tell him there's a mandatory two-day waiting period.

Instead, I pick up the social worker's card. I walk around the house with it. Put it in my pocket. I call Trapp in from outside, rub his muddy paws with an old towel and dry his flanks and withers with long hard sweeps with the flat of my hands. I return to the living room and pick up the slender cedar branch with those geese-shaped pinecones. Then I loft them into the air and watch them fly a moment against the gray sky through the window. When they fall they hardly make a noise on the wooden floor.

Maybe the social worker tells him that my mother is still incredibly unwell.

But maybe this isn't how it happens.

Maybe he cries, his body slumped against the hospital wall, his sobs shuddering through his shoulders.

But maybe he doesn't. Maybe it wasn't like that.

Maybe it was all completely different. And maybe I have a right to know how it was.

23

THE ADDRESS FOR THE 23RD STREET PROJECT takes us to one of Portland's older neighborhoods, one of wide avenues and stately run-down homes. Naked oak trees rustle above stone lions with their faces worn away and chipped urns flank the crumbling walkways and gates.

"Must have been some neighborhood," Neil says as the car rolls slowly along. We are arriving at dusk, the light has gone violet.

"What a waste. It's so run down now." The cars lining the streets are big junkers and the people walking along the sidewalks have the busy, blank faces of the working poor.

The house we want has scrollwork on the eaves, an ornately carved door, and a wraparound porch. Lattice grids climb between each floor. But the paint is chipped, the window frames and porch sag. Several garbage bins are lined up along the parking strip, one of them is tipped on its side with its contents spilling out onto the grass.

We check the number. We say nothing to each other. Two men stand together on the porch.

Neil turns off the engine. "Until college I thought half-way houses had something to do with the Underground Railroad."

"I thought they were for released criminals. A teacher told me something about them once but I misunderstood." I watch the men on the porch who are smoking, discussing something with broad hand gestures. I'm whispering now. "I thought they were for people who had committed a crime. And so this meant that my mother had done that."

Neil takes this comment quietly and does not acknowledge that I am telling him something I've never been able to tell him before. I do not say more, I do not say that even after I understood that a halfway house could also be a place to give former homeless a stepping-off point, I still believed my mother was a criminal.

We get out and walk toward the house. The men's postures shift as we approach and I know they've sensed our presence. One of them is wearing nothing but a t-shirt and his arms are blue from the cold. He has one cigarette in his mouth and another in his hand. In the semi-dark, the tip of his hand-held cigarette glows like the end of a stick of incense.

When we are only a few steps from the men, Neil stops and clears his throat a little. But he says nothing and I know I should be the one to speak. I open my mouth but I'm only thinking that I shouldn't mention my mother. This is a transitional place and it's been so long, no one who is here now will have known my mother when she lived here. My mother lived here, I think, instead of with me.

I stare at the men's jerky movements and their shapeless jeans. One man's hair is greasy, the other's is shaved. We are all staring at one another now. A door slams at the house next door and two cats sprint out from behind one of the garbage bins.

The man in short sleeves exhales smoke through his nose. "Just so you know, we're not interested in religion or charity." He laughs. "We're already up to our goddamn necks in charity."

"This is the 23rd Street Project?" Neil asks, but his voice is too quiet, he has to repeat himself. Both men nod with a kind of formal benevolence. "We're looking for someone named Erica Reza."

The men eye one another. The skinny man puts his hand-held cigarette between his lips so is now smoking both. He removes them, then says, "I don't know Erica."

The other man is dumpy, with skin that is pocked and scarred. He can't be much older than twenty. He stuffs his hands in his pockets, says, "She's not here anymore. She left."

The skinny, bare-armed man rolls his eyes and stomps a foot. "Man, you're always doing that. I feel *angry* when you do that."

"I was being honest. You can't ask me not to be honest."

"I was being honest. I *used* to know Erica. That means I don't know her anymore and I won't know her again until we re-acquaint ourselves through dialogue."

Neil shifts his weight, clears his throat again but the men continue.

"I believe I always know a person, just a little. I have the right to say I know them, even someone I haven't seen for a long time but used to know really well. Or even if we've just met and have only spoken for a few moments."

"Like the postal person?"

"Like the postal person." He swipes at the lank chunk of hair hanging over his forehead.

The sleeveless man gestures toward us with a flick of his index finger. "But you don't know them at all and yet now you've spoken."

He considers this, then turns his attention from the skinny man back to Neil. "Why are you looking for Erica?"

"Did she leave a long time ago? Do you know where she went or how to contact her?"

The men eye one another, the earlier challenge back in their eyes. The heavy one says, "She left this afternoon for her evening work at her office. She'll be back on Monday. She doesn't come on Thursdays and Fridays."

The skinny man hops up and down. "You see, man, you're always doing that. That makes me angry."

Before they can re-launch their earlier debate, Neil interrupts, "Can you tell us where her office is."

"We're not supposed to bother her at her office. We're supposed to resolve our conflicts without her intervention."

"If there's an emergency we have to call the walk-in clinic or the police."

A radio turns on in the house, somewhere on an upper floor. The music strikes out against the quiet cold air of the street. The skinny man lifts his head and mumbles something under his breath, then he whips a notebook from his back pocket, fishes for a little stub of pencil in his front pocket, and then he writes something down as my body chills with the memory of being in public with my mother, the shame of her note taking and constant suspicion.

Neil puts his hand to my lower back, stopping my slow retreat toward the car in a gesture that feels like an accusation.

"This is useless," I whisper. "They can't help us."

"They know this Reza woman."

"These men are unwell."

Neil's eyes darken. He removes his hand from where it was touching me.

"Why should we tell you about Erica?" the skinny man yells across the lawn. "We don't even know who you are."

Neil is still looking at me.

"They won't help us," I say. "They're on a different planet."

I have been whispering but Neil answers me in a normal voice,

"You are going to have to try harder than this." He turns and speaks to the men. "My wife's mother used to live here. She's missing and we're trying to find her. Erica might know where she is."

The heavyset one breaks rank with the skinny one, heads toward us. He is much bigger when he arrives, as tall as Neil. Even his beard is greasy and he smells of sour sweat. But his teeth are perfect. White and orderly. Shining "You should have said so in the first place." He points to a building attached to the big house. "Her office is on the second floor. She's normally there until six o'clock."

It is only just after 5:00 PM but she is already leaving as we approach the office door—we find ourselves face to face with a woman, a nameplate nailed to the door casing beside her shoulder. She has turned her head quickly upon hearing our footsteps and strands of her long black hair catch on the nail. Bright eyes behind spectacles. Long streaks of gray at her temples. She could be the twin of the first lab technician I ever worked with, a woman named Jamila, a woman who once lifted a greyhound's enlarged heart with her bare hands during an autopsy and held it up to my face—"drugs, far too many horrible drugs in this animal!"—that I stare too long without speaking.

Neil steps right in, asks her what we need to know and gives her my mother's name like it is any ordinary person's name.

The woman blinks. Glances from Neil to me, back to Neil, but quickly back to me. Too quickly. "You're talking about quite some time ago, yes?"

"We have some letters, reports, I think, that you wrote to Maggie's husband, John?"

She nods slowly, I can tell she is studying my face and then she blinks, looks back to Neil. "Yes, I remember. I remember Maggie Tomlinson."

Neil asks whether she has a few minutes for us, apologizes to catch her like this at the end of her day.

She checks her watch, gives us a tight smile. Then she ushers us inside and leads us down a narrow hallway. The walls of the hallway are covered in framed photographs, squares of mostly different shades of blue. I have to squint to see that they are pictures of the ocean—calm oceans, small waves, bordered by a long strip of sand. The stark calm of these pictures disconcerts me and I close my eyes against them.

She opens a door at the end of the hall and then we are inside a high-ceilinged room with armchairs and a messy desk. An aquarium fills half of it, its light casting a soft green glow upon the floor.

We introduce ourselves around, as if we haven't already done this outside. Hand shaking. Eye contact. I feel her eyes along my face and must look away.

"Please sit," she says, gesturing to her chairs. Neil sits. "And please call me Erica. This is certainly taking me back a few years. And it's a first."

"A first?" There is a smile in Neil's voice and I know he can't help this. This is what being polite sounds like. This is small talk. This is how life works.

Erica smiles at Neil. Glances at me. "I've never had family members come to talk to me so many years after a resident has left."

"Do you remember much about Maggie?"

She bobs her head left and right. "That's a difficult question to answer. I won't have her file anymore." And then she invites me to sit down one more time. This time I do. "I remember all our residents, especially the ones like Maggie,"—she glances at me—"who stay for several years."

The walls of her office are covered in the same blue photographs.

"We couldn't tell from your reports how long she was here."

"Three years. The maximum allowed."

She looks at me, as if I'm next in line for a question. I reach into my coat pocket, fishing for her card, like I need to show her some kind of proof. How we found her. Why we're here. Neil turns to me now as well. When I say nothing, when I only place her card on the desk and fold my hands back in my lap, Neil lets out a little puff of air, like's he's just reached the stop of a short, steep hill. She stands then and pours water into a small electric kettle. We are all silent as the kettle heats, as she takes three tea cups from a cupboard. She doesn't ask us if we'd like some, or what kind we'd like. When the water is ready, she pours it slowly and the sound of the pouring fills the room.

Handing us our tea, she says, "What brings you here?" Her slender fingers brush mine as I take the cup from her. "I hope Maggie isn't back on the streets, is that why you've come? Unfortunately, once you've lived in the house and left you cannot come back, it's just one of our rules, although I might be able to give you the names of some similar institutions."

Neil crosses and uncrosses his legs, holding his tea cup a little aloft. I watch him, waiting for him to speak again but he's staring at the ceiling, holding his gaze just above the two of us and he does not turn to meet my eye.

My palms are clammy with the fact that I must say something. I concentrate on a notched scratch on her desk, just where the joints in the wood make a neat angle. Then I look up and say, "You don't happen to know a woman named Jamila Nasar do you?"

Neil turns to me. Erica smiles and shakes her head.

And so I take a deep breath and I manage it. "We hoped you might be able to help us find her." Pause. Pause longer. Then, "Because my dad just passed away."

Erica closes her eyes and nods her head. I appreciate this acknowledgement and I take a sip of my tea; it is bitter and scalding hot. It sears across the roof of my mouth and I know I will lose little bits of skin.

Then I say, "And so we're trying to find her—"

"So she is back on the streets?"

"Well, no. Actually, we don't know."

Erica sighs, "I hate to think of her homeless again. I mean, I'm realistic about these things. I'm practically immune. But it isn't easy. I try not to be overly optimistic when someone gets back on their feet, because I know they often go back to what's more comfortable."

Erica seems to anticipate our surprise at this statement because she holds her hands out to us, fingers up, just briefly. "For people with mental illness, being ill is often more comfortable—even if it's harmful, even if it causes incredible damage. It is what it feels like to be that person."

I run my hands down my jeans and watch several short dog hairs float off into the air, then I find I cannot stop brushing them off. Smoothing the fabric along my thighs.

Neil says, "Do you have any idea where we might start looking for her? Your name is the first we came across when going through John's things."

She shakes her head. "I'm really sorry, but no. Some residents keep in touch and I'm happy when they do, but there's no obligation on either side. Thinking back on it, Maggie left the Project house for an alternative experiment. But I don't know what that experiment was. I remember that she was very excited. She was also a challenging resident. Not hugely different from others with similar disorders, but unique in her own way. I certainly didn't know everything about what happened when she was here, and so, no, nothing after she left."

"Why wouldn't she have told you?"

"Maggie was a very secretive person. This is quite common for someone with delusional disorder."

Neil's body comes to attention.

I hear my father's voice. Delusional disorder. Two words he gave me sometime after she left. Two words which rolled so easily around on my tongue, even at such a young age, two words which gave me visions of muddy floods and messy rooms.

These are words I've been avoiding, I realize, and with the thought comes a kind of relief. To my surprise I can suddenly evaluate the state of the animal in my presence: fearful, ashamed, seeking release in violence.

Erica continues, "Most individuals with delusional disorder will find a way to function. In the absence of great stress, or if certain triggers don't get triggered, they can live along a continuum of normalcy."

"What kind of triggers?" Neil asks.

She tips her head, "They're different for everyone. Fundamental triggers like stress or great trauma are pretty universal. But it's hard to know what can be stressful for someone—professional stress, family stress. A combination of factors."

"Do you know what Maggie's triggers were?"

"We don't work that way here, we work on coping, on day-to-day social skills. Triggers are a complicated thing. If someone has an obvious trigger, like an extreme agoraphobia, for example, we'll address it. But that isn't how it works for most people."

"My mother wasn't agoraphobic."

Erica nods. "No, she wasn't. Whatever her triggers were, she worked here on separating delusions from reality. She made progress." After a pause, she continues, "I'm curious, what was she like before she left?"

It takes me a moment to find the words, and all I can say is, "I remember it was like having two mothers." But this isn't what I want to say. I want to be able to quantify it, count up the months or years between the Before and the After and explain how she changed. Tell them about the borderland. But I just remember the boats, my dad in his wheelhouse, my steady walk forward. "I was ten when she left. It's a long time ago."

"I'm sure it's hard to remember."

Neil asks, "But how was she when she left here?"

Erica looks thoughtful. "Like I said, Maggie was challenging in certain ways. She kept herself apart from nearly everyone because she tended toward persecutory-type delusions. She had a complicated system that worked for her that was about controlling her information. This helped her feel safe. She didn't want to tell people too many things about herself."

"She made up stories," I say, and I don't mean for this statement to sound like I am shouting.

Erica stops. "Not exactly. Sometimes, yes, because individuals with delusional disorder interpret their world in a very particular way. It's like sense-making gone wrong, isn't it? By the time Maggie got here— you must know all our residents transition from a full-time institution first—she was already functioning."

"What does that mean?"

Neil has asked this but I also want to know. Does it mean she went back to the woman she had been when I was a child? The funny, eccentric one with the outlandish imagination? And if this was the case, why didn't I get to see her again?

"She was judged competent to live semi-independently."

"So she was cured essentially?" Neil says.

Erica draws her lips in a tight line. "We try not to think of mental health in those terms. People get better. They get worse. They manage. That cycle is constantly repeated over an entire life."

"I read your progress reports, the ones you sent to my dad, it seemed …"

"That she made headway? She did. She took some control over her behaviors before leaving. And she addressed her hearing problems."

Here I stop. "Hearing problems?"

Erica cocks her head. Her face is a question.

"My mother never had hearing problems," I say, my eyes darting around the room. Maybe we've all made a mistake and this isn't the right place after all.

"The Maggie Tomlinson who lived here for three years was almost completely deaf in her left ear. This presented a lot of challenges for her. Are you saying she wasn't deaf when you were a child?"

I shake my head.

Erica is thoughtful. "That's surprising. Her deafness contributed a lot to her delusional frameworks. Are you sure?"

"I'm sure," I say, but at the same time, I'm trying to think back. What am I really sure of anymore? I tilt, ever so slightly. I see her hands hovering at her cheek bones, her shouting, the way she tipped her head to listen. I hear her, "Look!"—was she always looking because she could not hear?

"Her deafness isolated her quite a lot. She enjoyed that, I think, but it also meant that she had trouble reading social situations. But she did address that while she was here. She understood she had to wear her hearing aid, she had to give people the benefit of the doubt at times, in case she misunderstood something. She would not have been able to leave if she hadn't addressed these things."

She pauses, then says, "But it's a lifelong struggle. And since she wouldn't really tell me where she was going, since she maintained the same level of secrecy even toward the end of her time at the house, I can assume she may have gotten worse as easily as I can assume she continued to manage things."

Neil is rubbing his forehead now, bouncing his leg up and down. I watch the nervous energy build inside him. He stands and walks to the walls of the room, begins to inspect these blue photographs.

"The residents take them. Just before they're ready to move out we go to the beach for the day. One on one. Wait," she says, getting up. "Maggie took one of these. This one here, no, maybe this one." She debates between two photos and I stand to see better. But I can tell right away which once would have been taken by my mother. It is a large scale sweep of blue, not a shoreline like most of the others, and in the far left corner, off in the distance and very small, there is a ferry.

Erica turns from the photos then and asks, "But why are you trying to tell her about your dad's death?"

This I am not expecting. This should be obvious. I touch the miniature ferry with my finger.

Neil says, "It seems they were in contact for all these years. Maybe even back together in some kind of relationship. We found her name listed on some property."

Erica cocks her head. "Really? That's unexpected."

I freeze.

"You do know John refused most contact with Maggie while she lived here? I sent him those updates on her progress because he felt it was better these things went through me. He managed the material and administrative side of certain things, and Maggie was judged competent enough after her years here that she was never placed under state or family supervision. Despite my encouragement on both sides to get back in contact, they only saw each other once that I know of when John brought her some clothing and personal belongings. And I believe they rarely spoke. Because of his stance I assumed they would never re-connect."

I take my hand from the photo. Turn my back to it. A quiet joy ignites inside me.

"Thank you," I say. "Thank you." And I mean this. I'm so grateful to get at least a few years of my dad's life back for myself. What a selfish and petty accomplishment, I know, but one which does not keep me from experiencing a triumphant relief. A grateful and giddy realization that I have not been entirely wrong about my own history.

24

WHAT IF THEY MET OUTSIDE, WHAT IF SHE is sitting on the front porch of the Project house. Maybe she's reading, her head bent over a book and her finger stuck between one of the back pages. If she doesn't see him approach, then for the briefest of moments maybe my dad can take a long look at her, remember her. I see him pretending for just a second.

I've heard the story of how they met at a dance for the Scandinavian society, I've heard about the blue dress she wore and her smile and her outrageous stories. I see him remembering how she pointed at a couple dancing across the room and said, "Get those two, they're related but they don't want anyone to know. They must be cousins and neither could find a real date."

"What makes you say that?"

"Come on, I know red hair and freckles when I see it. Only cousins could have that exact same color."

Maybe this memory makes him smile. But she's looked up now, and I see him stepping toward her, clearing his throat. Maybe there is a cane propped against the wooden railing, and maybe it startles him. Reminds him of everything that happened After. That he can't know about.

I see her flinching at his approach, because maybe she flinches when anyone walks up the steps toward the house. But maybe her flight stalls when she recognizes him. Maybe she tips her head to hear his approach and so he knows he can speak to her.

This is the part I can't really work out, though, no matter how many times I think about it. Is she happy to see him? Is she scared of him? Who is she by now?

She's in her fifties and her hair is still long. Maybe she's twisted it up, maybe it's in a ponytail. She will not stand up to return his greeting, and my dad will be relieved that he won't have to witness the extent of her handicap. He would have felt somehow responsible. I know this about him. My father is also in his fifties and I see the flecks of gray in his beard, his blue slacks and flannel shirt.

I know that no matter what, he will offer a polite hello and hand over the bag with her clothing and belongings. Maybe he gives her a stack of her once-favorite books. Her gardening manuals if he still had them. I imagine he will have prepared a stack of documents, too, things we kept that once belonged to her parents and uncles. Maybe a few photographs.

I see her taking these things quietly, setting them beside her. But maybe she doesn't. Maybe she wants nothing of his gifts.

Maybe he asks her how she's doing. Maybe she finds a way to answer him, twisting a piece of thread from the cuff of her sweater. "I don't have the same kind of brain as you do. That's really the hardest part. Do you have any idea what it's like to know your mind isn't to be trusted?"

My dad will shake his head. Maybe he won't know what to say.

"It's unthinkable. That your brain might not be reliable. But even if you think something might not be right, you don't stop trusting your mind."

"You don't?"

"Of course not, this would be death."

But maybe they say nothing to each other at all. Maybe he passes her the belongings he's collected and they hardly even look at each other. Maybe they are like strangers and he walks away without looking back even once.

25

THE PAPERS ARE ON THE COUNTER BESIDE me and no one is picking them up. We all know what they are, delivered in an envelope this morning from the printer. We are drinking our coffee and fussing with our clothing and we are nearly ready to leave the house. We almost leave without them, until George puts a firm hand on my forearm and nods his head at me.

"You must. You must, Ella. It will be okay."

These papers we have had printed for my dad's memorial service this morning. A program. As if this could be a thing that might exist. We have made an agenda around my dad's death and this makes no sense at all, as if bible verses and music and quotations might express what his life was about. I picture myself ripping this program into shreds of paper and dropping them from the deck of a ferry into the ocean. Below me are the smelt and the cat sharks and the herring and the gobies, and they swim through these disintegrating papers, around them, over, and maybe only then from those sea-drenched pieces of paper pulp we could tell the story of my dad's life. Of the salt-spray in his face and the line of dark trees and mountains inside his gaze. Of his body at the helm, his arms tugging on a fishing rod. Of his quiet mornings on the ocean, of his alone.

I hold onto these papers, hoping to dispose of them, somehow, but Neil has turned himself to face me and George is shaking his head and both their sets of eyes contain the same quiet as my dad's and so I don't rip anything. I give in and tuck the stack of bulletins into my bag while George locks the door, while Neil puts the dogs in the back yard, while I walk out of the house and down the lawn and stand by the car thinking that I should go back inside the house and turn off the lights upstairs. Aren't they on? Now I cannot tell anymore. Instead, I stay still, and I hold tight to these death programs and the only thing I can do is make one final pact with my mother, wherever she is. If she has seen our obituary, if she saw the small article the newspaper ran in tandem, if she is at all aware of what has happened, I tell her that she can come to the service this morning as long as she does not cry. Her grieving cannot rival my own. I simply won't allow it.

But she isn't there. I'm sure because I check for her in each group of mourners. I study wave after wave of the sad-faced people who enter the church and take their seats. The music is like a hush, while a wash of grays and blues and blacks fills the pews in a steady stream. Only the ferry crew members cannot help their brightness. The gleaming buttons on their jackets, the bright stripes on their shoulders, the flash of gold on their hats. There are so many of them; it seems like the entire Washington State Ferry service has turned out for my dad's memorial.

Neil and I sit in front, with George and Lisa. Behind us is my dad's First Mate and several other captains with their wives and families. Compared to the solid ranks of them, our pew seems empty.

Despite the fact that I am here, that this is happening, I cannot seem to keep my mind focused. I am about to experience my dad's memorial, I remind myself.

This is where you are, Ella. This is today.

I watch everyone with their programs in hand. I'm holding one, too. I try to read it, but the words just swirl together. I put it beside me on the seat—right on top of the box of my dad's ashes that I placed inside a canvas bag and took from the house this morning, worried that leaving him behind for the service would be somehow careless or, worse, impolite. I keep my hand on top of the bag for a moment, but this doesn't help me focus either.

I have only attended one other funeral—Nana's—when I was fourteen. That service was nearly cheerful. All those old ladies, a sprinkling of old men, carrying on and on and telling each other stories. Stories about Nana doing this or that at some church picnic, about how nice the pastor's message was, how he described Nana's quick wit so perfectly. Mostly, though, I remember that they talked about their bodies and their illnesses and medicines. They compared aches and injuries, and I found this all so sad. I remember feeling so relieved that Nana died in such good health.

At that service, I remember my dad was sedate but not too upset, kind and polite to all the elderly couples, and he'd even joked with George about one of the women.

"Do you see who that is?"

"I don't believe it."

The woman in question had a crown of bright white hair and was nearly bent in half. She was dressed formally, down to a pair of white lace gloves, hat, and sparkling brooch.

"She was 100 years old when we were kids."

"Agnes Johansson," my dad said. "She's been a widow for more than sixty years. Imagine that."

I remember them both growing quiet. My dad tucking his chin.

George looking away. My dad was as good as a widower, and I knew someday someone might say the same thing about him.

The service is surprisingly short. We sing a few hymns, listen to a scripture reading, Pastor Tim gives a short message. George and another of the ferry captains deliver two separate eulogies. I hover above it all as though the person they are talking about is someone I knew only briefly. Or someone I knew a long time ago. If I don't talk to you tomorrow, then I won't know you anymore until we re-acquaint ourselves through dialogue.

Pastor Tim stands up and announces that John Tomlinson was a great man, that we will surely miss him, that we will all remember him with "a reflection of his good nature in our hearts." I nearly stand up and say that reflections are for magicians but instead, I hold the fingers of my right hand tightly in my left hand. He makes a final prayer that I try to mimic with my lips, as if this might help me. That maybe just by saying it all, I will feel some of its effect. And then the organist is playing and there is a line of people to let pass before me, shake hands with. People are so incredibly kind. Some of the women are crying. Most of the other ferry crew members—a line of men, their eyes conspicuously wrinkled from their days on the sea—are predictably stoic. Only Jonathan, my dad's First Mate of many years, pulls me into his arms. He squeezes me so tight that I can hardly breathe. And the hug lasts so long that I begin to get used to it, I relax my shoulders and drop my head into the natural indent at his shoulder. I can smell his shirt beneath my nose, can smell something like kitchen grease and a whiff of coffee. He is trembling and this makes me begin to shake, too. When he finally lets go, he just walks away without a word, without a goodbye.

Lisa is holding my hand, and I don't even notice this until I see that George has gone on ahead toward the back of the church and the reception that is planned downstairs. His duck boots clomp along the floor, echoing on the stone walls.

"Come down when you're finished," she says, dropping my hand and walking quickly to catch up with George.

Neil waits with me until everyone has filed past and headed downstairs.

"George said some of the mates have invited us for food, after the reception, I mean."

"I think I'd rather just go home."

His voice quiets. "It's what people do, Ella. After something like this. They gather together. Keep each other company."

I lean my head back to see his face. I note the shadows under his eyes, the slope of his nose. No longer just stubble, a real beard is forming along his jaw. His lips are chapped and rough and I reach a finger to my own, smooth across the skin.

"People will want to support you," he says. "Make sure you're okay."

This stops me. "Are you okay?"

We are nearly alone in the church now. He folds his arms, clasping his right hand under the opposite elbow. His knuckles whiten. "I'll tell them to wait for you."

I watch Neil move away from me into the tide of well-wishers. There he goes, each step a measurable distance from myself. A pew. Two pews. Three pews. And then, to equal parts grief and relief, the back of his head suddenly seems so decided, so distinctly turned away. I've done it, I think. I've done what needs to be done. My first appointment is tomorrow.

I stay alone in the church with only the organ music floating around me. The organist is still playing, slogging through a quiet recessional with muted low notes. The notes bounce off the church's brick walls and stained-glass windows. I sit myself down in the first pew to wait out the song, and see that I have left the box of my dad's ashes in its lonely patch of velvet-covered pew. I pick it up and set it on my lap, spread my hands flat across the canvas-covered wood.

When I was six years old I fell off a swing set at a park. I'd been with George, I remember this so clearly because he'd taken me out for pizza and this was such an unusual treat. On the way home from the restaurant we stopped at Golden Gardens so I could play. I remember asking him to push me higher, I remember wanting to show off for him. And then I remember only the sudden lightness of my body, the dizziness in my head and belly as I slipped forward into the air, out of the swing seat, and then the awful thud as I hit the ground on my back. I could not speak, I could not breathe. I remember George's face—its small tight mouth, his startled eyes—above me. It was like my lungs had collapsed inside of me, the thin membranes sticking together. I remember the panic, the awful choking panic.

I look at the box of my dad's ashes and my lungs are collapsed again. I want to breathe. I want the in and out of air that means that I am moving forward, moving away from this awful stuck moment. But the air just won't come. I try and I try. Nothing. I feel my face growing red, I feel a kind of gasp welling up inside my chest. But nothing. The organist isn't playing her recession anymore, but something rapid and light. Something Baroque. But the speed of her fingers and feet cannot get my breathing working. The music moves quickly and my panic speeds up to meet it.

"I'd like to say a quick word," comes a voice beside me. "If I may?"

Here is the face of an old woman leaning down toward me—through my panicked gasping, I mark out a pointy chin, tightly coiffed steel-gray hair, small moles along the cheek.

She sits down beside me. Her hair is so gray it is more like lilac. I am getting lightheaded now, praying I'll manage an intake of breath.

I stare at her.

"Here, take this," she says, pulling a handkerchief from her purse.

I try to speak. Only squeaks come out of my throat.

Then her face gathers itself, her eyebrows move against one another and starts thumping my back with a small bony hand. She just hits and hits and it hurts, I feel a burst of pain thread across my shoulders but she keeps hitting me and all at once my 6 year-old self is flying backward into the air, back to the swing and I am moving forward again, cradled in the sound of the organ music floating through the quiet church.

"Thank you," I say, embarrassed now. My eyes darting down and up to this woman's face.

She retrieves her handkerchief and folds it neatly in her lap. "You'll be alright in a moment." She swivels her head, takes in the church. "A bit bright, isn't it? Aren't churches supposed to be a little darker?"

I nod my agreement. I have thought this since stepping inside this morning.

"But nothing like that could keep me away. He was my captain, you see."

What an odd thing to say and I tell her so.

"Oh, yes. I live on Bremerton. And your dad even knew my grandchildren, you see. They ride with me sometimes. I take care of them a lot." She huffs, and traces a fingernail with the pad of her thumb. Her hands are arthritic and knobby. I want to reach over and smooth out one of her bent knuckles.

"He knew your grandchildren?" Ferries are not like buses where everyone greets the driver and other commuters. Ferries keep their captains hidden away in the wheelhouse. Barred from public access by thick chains and locked doors.

The woman continues, "Your dad was very kind. He let me ride up top nearly every time."

I stare at this woman. I always ride with the crew. Walking on with my dad a few minutes before the passengers load, finding a comfortable seat for myself in the row of bank seats behind the captain's control deck. I try to quell the sting, the childish jealousy, at the thought of someone else getting preferential treatment besides myself.

"Yes," the woman giggles, her bright eyes mischievous.

I say nothing. A vague memory wiggles at the back of my brain. My dad laughing and telling me during one of our weekly phone calls of an older lady who insisted she ride with the crew to make sure they weren't sleeping or drinking on the job. My dad thought she was hilarious.

"He was always gracious," this woman is saying. "He never argued with me. Not like some of the other captains. I wasn't trying to be trouble."

I say nothing. I see him smile at her, hold out his big hand to shake hers and lead her up to the wheelhouse, grinning and knowing she will entertain him on the ride across the Sound. I want to be held by that hand, too. I want to walk up those stairs behind his familiar shape and size.

"I must tell you how happy I am to finally meet you," she says. "Your dad was very proud of you. You're all he ever talked about. I feel like I know all about you. I've even heard some of your vet stories— you must be such a devoted veterinarian." I watch the woman's watery eyes dance across the altar, the pulpit, the wooden cross hanging in the apse of the nave. Her head nods a tiny bit each time her eyes alight on a new object.

And then her name lands in my mouth. "You're Mrs. Baumann."

"I knew he couldn't forget about me," she says, obviously pleased. Then her face smooths out. "I am so sorry about this accident. What a useless tragedy." She shakes her head and I grip that box of ashes.

"Yes," I whisper, feeling the ferocious edge of this tiny soft-sounding word.

"But you were always what we talked about," she says again.

The organist has finished that Baroque piece now and is launching into a prelude. She must be practicing, I realize, for another service or for next Sunday, and I am grateful for the reminder. Today will turn into tomorrow. And tomorrow into yet another day.

Mrs. Baumann scoots forward in the pew, leaning her body away from me. "I'll leave you, this is a quiet lovely place for you right now. But can you point me toward your mother? I couldn't quite make her out. I'd like to speak with her, too. Your dad told me so much about her. Was she that lovely woman with the flowers?"

"No," I say, surprised at how quickly I can push this word from my lips. What a futile pact I made with my mother before the service. Of course she was here all along. All of my life her absence has taken up more space than her presence. "No," I repeat. "Maggie's not here."

"Oh! She's not?" Mrs. Baumann fumbles with the cuffs of her dark jacket. "She's not here. Well, I suppose she didn't have time to come up from Oregon?"

I swallow her question, pull it with the movement of my tongue into a place that is deep inside of me.

Mrs. Baumann smiles lightly. "John told me all about the commune. He really was an open-minded man, I think. Veterinarian daughters and hippie wives. I shouldn't say that, though, you'll think I'm a sexist. But at my age, well, anyway." She pats her own hand with the other. She cocks her head at me. "It's such a hard day, isn't it? I lost my Andrew four years and three months ago. Even at my age it surprised me. Life is like that."

The church is perfectly quiet now. Silent. A commune?

"He never said so, you know, but I could just tell he wasn't happy at their separation. He wasn't a man to complain, though, was he?"

I place my forehead against the pew back in front of me. I feel the wood press against the flat plane of my skull. The address book with the ferry names. The *Champoeg*. There is no ferry named The *Champoeg*. I've had the names of the ferries memorized since I was a little girl, a fun game to please my dad when we had company. I think again about everything I found at the cabin. All those homemade items. The carved figurines, the hand-knitted scarf. And Erica Reza talked about an experiment.

The woman brings her hands together and worries the tips of her fingers. "I've upset you, haven't I? I just assumed she was your mother. John never said he'd been married twice. I didn't think she could be a first wife. Oh, these things are so complicated these days. I'm so sorry. And you've just called her Maggie."

I sit back up. I just stare at her.

"I'm so sorry. I should have been more careful. And of all days to put my foot in it."

"No," I say, stopping her protests with a hand on her hand. And then I do it, I admit that Maggie is my mother.

It is an extraordinary feeling to acknowledge a relationship you would rather deny. Hearing Mrs. Baumann's indulgent understanding of what she must feel was my mother's alternative lifestyle brings me back to my teenage self. The lies and omissions I handed my friends and teachers whenever the dangerous subject of my mother came up. The daydreams I could not help but entertain about what it would be like to come home, just once, to a healthy woman who might ask me about my day, sit down in front of the TV with me, take me for a walk along the beach, or pass me a book she had just finished reading.

"Why didn't he tell me?" I ask Mrs. Baumann, still gripping her papery hand.

Her eyes twitch. "Tell you what, dear?"

"Why didn't he ever say?"

Mrs. Baumann sits up and swivels her head toward the back of the church. When she turns back to face me, she pulls her hand away and says, "This is always the hardest day. Let's get you downstairs."

26

So what if it's all as simple as I've believed all along. She left, she became another person. And so maybe she lives in a log cabin with a group of pot smokers. Maybe she's now changed her name to Wisteria and wears her hair in two fiery red braids that fall all the way down her back and swing when she walks, which is barefoot, through the forest, singing to the birds, attending ceremonies with other teepee-dwellers during the full moon. Look at her—she's so down-to-earth, so in tune with the movement of the clouds and the timing of the weather, the cycles of the harvests, the animals (no, not the animals, those are mine), the turning of the seasons, the growth of the food and the forests.

Maybe she takes a vow of silence each year for months at a time, saying goodnight to her friends at midnight on the 21st of December and keeping absolutely quiet until the 21st of June, when she'll walk out to a river and sing a song of forgiveness to the earth, when her voice will sound oily and harsh until she's managed a few verses and then, when they hear her, her friends will join in and that day at the commune will be noisy and filled with stories. Does she still know how to tell stories? Has she told them her own?

Maybe she has lived in this cabin for several years, maybe she makes her own clothes out of bartered or recycled cloth and wool that she spins with the other men and women, knitting it in the mornings before an open fire in this communal camp. Do they read books together? Do they pray? Do these community members take hallucinogenic mushrooms once every two months on a day they have designated Mind Day. And when they trip all together in their clearing near their camp, what do her trips contain? Maybe she's sees my dad and remembers what it was like to stand in the boat with him, her hand on his forearm, while the boat chuffed and skimmed the waves. Maybe her heart still races, her feet spread wide to keep her balance. And maybe, just maybe, in her drug-addled trips she remembers—just for a second, just long enough for the spark to fly from brain to nerve to belly—a little girl who looked just like her, whose hand held hers back, who always listened when she said, "Look!" and who followed. Who always, stupidly, followed.

"Look," she says to her friends.

They look, their eyes glassy but trying.

No one can see where she's pointing. No one can see the face that's floated across the inside of her mind. And it doesn't matter because it's all gone so quickly. The reminder. The memory. A good thing, too, because there are chores to be done, food to be gathered and cooked, plants to praise, spices to grind. What is the ghost of a face when there is so much real goddamn work to be done?

27

MY FIRST SURPRISE OF THE EVENING—we are at a restaurant, we are "celebrating" my dad's life—is George and how he shape-shifts and changes size. Usually such a small contained person, I watch his shoulders straighten with each "John would have ..." and his body grow taller with each "John loved ..." It doesn't matter who says these things, they are all somehow coming from or directed at George. They surround him while we eat at two long tables covered in a fisherman's feast. His arms move and his hands dance, and he parcels out his entire friendship up and down the table to the nods and smiles and tears of everyone listening.

It's like he's breaking off pieces of memory and tossing them out—a weekend of fishing here, a hike to Anderson Lake here, a joke at a ball game, a near emergency at the Vashon pier, a car accident when they were teenagers. He gives it all, and the more he talks, the more impossible it seems for him to stop. He's going over their entire relationship, he's reliving it.

He continues to expand across the evening—and for the first time since I've known George and Lisa as a couple, George is taking up all the space. His newly broadened shoulders radiate a kind of demented joy. There's an edge to him, but he's so glorious it doesn't matter. Everyone wants to be near him. Everyone wants to hear him. I do, too. His stories feel like hot water on my skin but I can't seem to pull myself from his orbit, even laughing at all the right moments, nodding in corroboration if he asks me to.

"Remember?" he says.

"I remember," I say.

"Remember?" he says to Lisa, or to Neil.

"I remember," they say.

Everyone is smiling. I'm smiling, too. But my smiling feels like a muscle movement, like something my face is doing on its own, with no connection to how I'm really feeling. So I watch everyone else, too. Are their smiles genuine? I think they are. I pick up my napkin and I wipe it carefully across my lips. Then I use it to sweep bread crumbs from the table to the floor. This is a really nice restaurant. The freshest fish. The most flavorful herbs.

When we leave the restaurant and move to a nearby brewery, a place my dad used to stop by on his way home from work, I watch George grow even taller until he seems to tower over the other ferry captains and mechanics and able-bodied seamen. He tells the loudest stories, laughs with his entire body, accepts hugs from strangers, and dances with Lisa when she brings him a beer. This is when I know his grief is no longer lodged firmly in his spine. Tonight isn't some fluke of emotional exhaustion. His body has lightened. He's figured out how to make these two parts of his life—the one with my dad, and this new one without—touch at some point that he can actually see now. It will take all his storytelling, and all his good cheer, but they will fit. Someday they will feel seamless. This is when I can't stand to be near him anymore. I'm not angry with him, but my own spine is still housing an unwanted guest.

As I'm moving away, Lisa reaches for me. "It's going to be okay, Ella." So I know she's noticed it, too. Her relief is palpable. She won't have to worry so much about him anymore.

I nod at her. I think, sure, it's going to be okay.

But my second surprise of the evening comes when Neil hands me the car keys, sees the beer in my hand, and says, "You probably shouldn't finish that." My glass is completely full.

His face is smooth in the dim light and a shadow on his cheek makes it seem like he's actually smiling. His blonde hair is ruffled, a bit too long because he was due for a haircut already last week. For a moment we are students again, we've just met in a Cell Biology course and I'm thrilled to run into him outside of the classroom. For a moment, we hardly know each other and we're about to sit down together and begin a conversation that doesn't stop until three in the morning, until we're leaning in so close our margins have blurred. For a moment, I want only to stand so close that I can feel the heat from his arm radiating across to mine. But he doesn't stay to talk to me, he just hands me a glass of water and walks out into the crowd. Our margins are completely distinct.

I watch him with a group of crew members—their white uniforms still bright, unwrinkled, despite the hours they've been wearing them. And Neil seems to fit in so well here. Everyone knows him. All these people. There are so many people here to celebrate my dad's life: men and women and even some children. Face after face after face. And I think how I should know these people. Some of them talk to me, and maybe I answer them in the right way. Nod when they say, "I'm so sorry," and put on a good face when they ask how I'm doing.

I say, "I'm hanging in there."

I say, "Thank you so much for coming."

I say, "Gathering like this is exactly what he would want."

At some point, I lose track of Neil completely. But when I think enough time has passed and I could excuse myself and go home, he is nowhere to be found. I walk around the bar several times, back and forth, until George sees me, stops me.

"I can't find, Neil," I say.

George furrows his brow. "He left already. He said you knew."

So I nod and say, of course I knew, I'm just tired. Then, "It's been a long day."

I watch George and he's still so tall. So filled up with his movement forward. He can look me in the eye, his eyes brimming with the good memories he's relived this evening. A light from the bar paints his cheek red, and all I can think about is Mrs. Baumann's white hair as we walked out of the church, how it changed color in the stained glass.

George calls over to Lisa and I know they're lying, but they say they're ready to go and offer to drive me home. But I've got the car keys anyway. I jiggle them, smile and say, "No need. I've got the car."

"But Neil," says Lisa, her mouth open, trying to sort it out.

"It's okay," I say. "It will all work out."

"What will work out?" she says.

When I don't answer, she follows me, her skirt swishing, her scarf trailing behind her. I turn back to her, take her scarf and knot it once around her neck.

"There," I say, "Don't lose this."

"Ella … ?" she seems to shout, but I am already turned around and headed out the door.

Out into the night then, and for the first time in days it isn't raining, and there's no wind. The sky is perfectly black. I breathe deep. It is always there—the smell of the ocean, the seaweed and the salt. I stand next to my car for some time, breathing. I see two more people I should know—is that Leonid? I don't think I could ever forget those arms and his great beak of a nose—walking out of the door but they don't see me. No one sees me where I'm standing in the darkness. I'm there, but I'm not there at all.

The *Champoeg*. How clever this was, Captain. Hiding her information where anyone could see it.

When I get back to my dad's house—which is empty, as I've expected it to be—the first thing I do is Google the phone number listed after The *Champoeg*. It's so easy. In only a few seconds I've got the listing for *Friends' Farm*, an intentional community twenty minutes southeast of Eugene. Its website is sparse but it's clearly a farming and living collective, like so many that still dot the Pacific Northwest. There are no member names listed, no pictures of the people. Only a series of bright photographs of artfully arranged piles of produce arranged by season. Fall: dozens of squash varieties, a U-pick pumpkin patch, heirloom zucchinis. Winter: loose leaf Christmas tea spread across white linens, cinnamon candles. Spring: wildflower bouquets, woven baskets filled with honey pots, bunches of tulips and daffodils. Summer: U-pick berries by the bucketful held up by hands stained pink and purple. The website offers two things in writing besides the directions: a guarantee—*All our produce is 100% organic and both planted and picked with care*—and a warning—*All transactions must be made in cash.*

I don't call the number. I put my phone down and sit in the living room, my dad's ashes in their box beside me on the couch, and I wait for Neil. I wait for Neil with the palms of my hands cupped over my aching breasts. My body is doing so well, I think, doing what needs to be done. I feel nearly sorry for it; its work will be interrupted and it will have to adjust. Around 2:00 AM, I wake with a start, still on the couch, my neck and right shoulder stiff. The house is silent. The dogs are curled up on the floor at my feet. I listen with my whole body, but I can tell this house is perfectly silent. Neil isn't here. I stand for twenty minutes trying to compose a text to him but eventually I turn off my phone and crawl into bed.

But I've missed my window. Whatever sleep my body needed, it accomplished while I was on the couch. I lie still and I catalog my body—my legs under the sheets, my hip bone pressed against the mattress, my arms tucked up under my face. My limbs are heavy, my skin feels dry. I am contained beneath this sheet, the shape of me a solid and heavy object. I try and I hope and I breathe, but I cannot pretend I don't feel it. This heat in my lower abdomen, the constant pull of nausea.

A cell cluster. A mass of tissue.

I told a client once: "Any embryo is hell-bent on life. It will grow faster than you imagine."

If the owner isn't breeding their animal, I always recommend sterilization before any chance of insemination. It's so much easier on the mother dog or cat or cow or horse. How many times have I said this to clients waiting out that first year? Dozens. Hundreds. And every week I perform this surgery. It is one of my favorites because it involves such perfect efficiency. In vet school we learn about this. What is the most efficient way to close a body after surgery? If we are careful we can control the functioning of a scar. How it will manifest itself both within and on the outside of an injury. Despite its potential length, depending on the animal, one of the easiest scars to manage is the one following sterilization. This makes it my favorite. Because the scar I craft will vanish completely. It isn't a complicated procedure, and only involves a double closure, inner stitches and outer staples. These two layers knit together so that when the staples are finally removed the skin unrolls, pink and delicate but perfectly smooth, leaving nothing but a hairless line down the delicate belly, softened by the surrounding rustle and tide of fur. As if the injury never happened.

My appointment is in five hours. I wonder when Neil is coming back.

I get up, shower, eat a bowl of cereal, walk around my dad's house, throw up the bowl of cereal. Drink a glass of water. Put on a sports bra instead of my normal bra. Eat a cracker.

My appointment is in four hours. I walk through the house, up the stairs and down the stairs and out into the backyard with the dogs, out onto the front lawn to look at the car, at the neighbor's houses. I eat another cracker. The sky is threatening rain again. Winter is so long here, I think. So wet and so dark. The animals have it right—migration, hibernation, adaptation. I could achieve torpor, I think. I could reduce and slow and hold it all in.

The sound of a car pulling up along the curb. My appointment is in three and a half hours. The sound of a car door. A voice. Neil's voice. "Thank you," he says. The sound of a car pulling away. The dogs are barking now, they've heard him.

The sound of footsteps in the driveway. The sound of a hand at our car parked in the driveway, but I've locked the door, so there is nothing but the click of the handle being pulled, dropped back in place. Then the gate opening.

There he is.

He looks at me. I look at him. He knows one thing about me today. This thing is on his face. What do I know about him? He raises a hand to his face, fingertips to his temple, elbow hard bent, like he's about to salute me. But the gesture falls apart and he says, "Give me the car keys."

I can hear in his voice that he's drunk. All six feet of him. Messy and sloppy and hard-alcohol drunk.

"You can't drive, Neil."

He laughs and his whole body slumps. Then rights itself with a small sway. "I don't want to drive," he says. "Just give me the keys."

"No."

"No, yourself. I want them all back. They're in the car."

"What are?"

But he shakes his head. "They're mine." His voice is loud, too loud. It doesn't sound like Neil. The dogs have shied away from him, are watching him from a distance.

"I'll get them myself," and he pushes past me up the steps and into the kitchen, returns with the keys. I don't stop him. As he walks past me, his arm brushes mine and the place where we touch retains the sensation of our touching. My arm moves without my permission, follows him but he's already at the gate. Out the gate. Opening the car.

I hear rustling. I cannot seem to get my feet moving. I've never seen Neil so drunk and there is something spectacular about it. So noisy and chaotic. Despite his tall frame, Neil is the kind of person who can enter a room without anyone noticing. But now every movement is signaled, outsized. I walk toward the gate, into the driveway and see him half in the passenger side door, his legs sprawled out the open door. He's throwing things over the door—a bright red maple leaf, a clutch of green ferns, a small white shell, rocks. These are my things. Objects he's given me that have collected in the car. His extraordinary gifts.

He yells, still throwing, "You're not going to ask me, so I'm just going to tell you." Another leaf floats down beside the car door. "I don't care, Ella. I'm telling you. Because everyone agrees. You're being unreasonable."

"Who is everyone?"

He waves this away. He's getting up now from the car. It's so loud, the shuffling of his feet on the gravel, the rustling of his coat as he removes it. His face is red, and he's carrying a small box. I recognize it but can't remember from where. I shake my head. His coat falls off his arm, he reaches for it but sways. "Every fucking person I spoke to."

I watch him.

"I've counted them up. Seventeen people. Men and women. Old and young. I even spoke to an old Chinese lady and she said I should leave you. She was clear about this."

"You told strangers about us?"

He holds a hand up. "Just shut up." He winces though, at the sound of these words. Looks up at the sky, bites his lip. "Do you want to know the best part?"

I say nothing.

"Wait. This is the best part. You can't have the other things, but you need this."

He holds the box toward me. Small. Plain.

He says, "Got the mail yesterday. Before the service. Didn't want to upset you." Here he laughs but it's an awful grating sound. "Isn't that amazing of me? I didn't want to upset you."

The box has a number on it. Written in pencil. Number 42.

"See," he says, opening the box. "It's all here." He pulls out a small map of the Puget Sound. A sailor's map. "This one," he says, handing me the map, "this one is for your dad. His name is written on it."

I take the map and unfold it. Re-fold it.

"And this one," he says, sitting down on the stoop, pushing the dogs back, rubbing his eyes. "You'll never fucking believe this, but this one is for me." He pulls out what appears to be two knitted socks. "It took me all night to figure out what the hell these are. You'll never guess."

He hands them to me. I have no idea what they are.

"No, no," he says. "Keep looking. It's amazing actually. They're so well knitted. They might actually work."

"What are they?"

"They came folded up, tied with twine and they had my name on them, Ella. My fucking name."

How dare she, I think, and I begin to shiver. Why can she know about my life?

"They're hiking gaiters. She made them for me. She signed the note."

He's nodding now, his face twisted and puffy. "Exactly. Creepy, isn't it? I thought so. So it throws everything upside down for you, doesn't it? Good. But they're beautiful. I'm actually going to use them when I go out to research. They'll be perfect. They'll keep my feet dry."

"This was in the mailbox?"

He nods, no longer smiling. "Should I have given these to you yesterday?"

I'm shaking with cold now, my teeth have begun to chatter.

"Here's the box. See for yourself. I need a shower before George and Lisa get here."

I check my watch. Yes, George and Lisa. We have one more task to accomplish today before I go to my appointment. Alone.

"Neil?" I say, but he's already getting up, shaking his head. He doesn't seem drunk anymore now. Not even a little.

He walks up into the house, but before he turns around he looks at me. I know what he's asking. Instead, I look into the box.

There's another item in the box. A small package of sterile surgical masks, and a leaflet from the CDC. My fingers reach for this stack of masks—once, twice, three times, but they fumble with the soft paper, drop them. I sit down on the stoop, put the box on my lap. There are little folded papers and bits of string; Neil has cut the strings, but the papers are clearly little tags: John, Ella, Neil. And then a larger folded paper. I open it: *Next box will be late, in six weeks. Number 43 will be late. Okay? And Hal says the 16th for the island, okay? Sincerely, Maggie Tomlinson.*

I turn the box over to check the date stamp while that wave crashes over me once again. The impossibility of her. The cold and the wet. The package was stamped in Eugene, OR, two days after my dad's accident.

28

WHEN GEORGE AND LISA ARRIVE, Neil and I are standing together on the front stoop. The dogs have each been given a rawhide bone to chew while we're away. George is driving, Lisa is putting chapstick on as their car pulls up to the curb. Neil and I don't move, waiting for their car to stop completely. From a distance we must look so well matched. His shoulders a few inches above mine, my head reaching so easily the space between his shoulders and his cheek. Our feet could be touching, my hand could quickly slip into his open hand.

Our hands are closed and we keep our attention on George and Lisa's clean silver Toyota. But then Neil says, "You're going today."

I nod, even if it wasn't a real question.

He doesn't turn to me but the air settles between us, gathers and grows dense. "To this clinic."

I shake my head now because I know it's my fault. "You know this, Neil. You know there's no other way," I say, shaking my head because I know it's my fault that our perfectly ordinary relationship has ended up in such disarray.

"You make no sense, Ella."

George and Lisa's car is stopped. The engine off. Their heads are turned to us. But we don't yet move.

"What if I say no?" Neil asks.

"We don't have a choice." And I'm ready to take a step down, to head toward the car that's waiting for us, but Neil stops me with a hand on my arm. Tight. His fingers close around my elbow and this is nothing like an embrace.

"You're kidding me. What do you mean by 'we'?"

I try to pull my arm from him. "I mean it."

"You are a free being and we are bound to each other and to ourselves and our ideas of right and wrong and whatever fucking else." Only now do I still hear the echo of slurring. He's still a little drunk.

By now George has opened his door and stepped out. Lisa rolls down her window, says, "Are you ready, my loves?"

I whisper to Neil then; my whisper is so fierce it surprises me. "None of this was supposed to happen."

His eyes narrow, he drops my arm. "Suppose we accept that it has."

"I accept it, Neil. You're the one asking me to change things," I say, but he's already walking toward the car, and he's the one carrying the bag with my dad's ashes inside, so I have nothing to do but follow.

In the car we exchange greetings. George is small again today, but there's a lightness to him. His shoulders have relaxed, his hands on the steering wheel are not holding anything but the car. He pulls out and we're on our way. We drive in silence.

Halfway to the pier, Lisa turns in her seat and gives us a smile that is both sad and radiant. But her forehead creases at the sight of us.

And she's right because Neil has had enough of our silence, "Tell me you've imagined it."

I stare at him.

"Just think about it. Imagine it. Him or her."

"Don't."

Neil's tongue stumbles over the words. "I figure the odds are stacked for red hair. And brown eyes. Long toes. Surely the kid would have long toes."

"I won't do this," I say.

"No, that's the problem. You will. You're telling me that you will."

Lisa's eyes widen. George glances at us in the rearview as Lisa tries to cut in, but the words are lost behind Neil's voice, rising in anger, "I've got a pretty deep voice. You think that sort of thing gets passed along?" He swipes at his eyes. His nostrils flare, the tips turning red.

"It's irresponsible," I say, closing my eyes against the little hands and smooth shoulders, the dip where the baby's spine curves into a neck.

"What is? Entertaining the possibility?"

"This whole thing is irresponsible. It's the genetics of it. I won't discuss this."

"Like hell you won't."

Lisa says, "My loves, you're scaring me. You're scaring both of us."

Neil says, "You will discuss it, you will talk to me about it."

"I won't."

Lisa tries again, "Neil, Ella … please. We can stop. We can talk."

"A child, Ella. This is not some small thing you can imagine away."

"I'm not imagining anything!"

George says, "Ella, honey?"

Lisa says, "Oh, lovies!"

But Neil talks over both of them, "Yes, you are. You're making everything up and you're getting it all wrong. You're completely deluded."

"Stop it!" I shout, putting my hands over my ears.

The car is silent. I've silenced everyone.

"Just stop it," I say, trying to move as far away from him as possible in the small car. The only sound is the rain on the roof and Neil's furious breathing.

George says, then, stiff and quiet, "Do we need to stop for a second?"

"We don't need anything," I say.

"We need everything," Neil says.

"Wait," Lisa says, "wait now, we're here," and the two of us look up to see the *Sealth* looming off the end of the pier, its gaping underside still empty.

"We need, shit, I don't know what we need." He's zipping and unzipping his jacket. Over and over. "We need a time-out, we need to draw a line and ..." But I close my ears to him. I fill myself with the view of this ferry, with the flat horizon of the water and the mountains in the distance. The water. The ocean. The ferries.

The line of cars is short and it only takes a few minutes for it to be our turn to drive up the ramp and follow the Loader's pointed arm toward the aisle he's assigning us. George parks the car and turns off the engine. Each of us opens a door. Each of us steps out and zips up a jacket, puts on a hood. This is the 10:15, my dad's morning run to Southworth, with a stop on Vashon. Neil is carrying my dad's ashes, and we climb the stairs single file to the third outside deck.

The ferry is not busy, and the people who are riding have mostly stayed inside. A handful of smokers, wrapped up in windbreakers and scarves, line the railing, watching the water as we get underway. We find a bench in a wind shelter just below the navigation deck but it doesn't keep the rain off. We tuck ourselves back as far as we can, seated in a row. George, then me, then Lisa, then Neil. We keep our faces to the water. We keep our shoulders squared. The rain is so thick it doesn't even seem like rain, it feels more like the ocean is heaving itself up and throwing itself back down. Like the water below us and the water falling from above are part of the same massive water system in the midst of a tantrum. In a few short moments my jeans are soaked. Everyone else is just as wet, but no one moves. We sit hunkered down on our bench like hardy seabirds. We draw sideways glances from passengers who have remained inside. Safe behind the thick glass.

The boat heaves itself forward, and I look south at those impossibly red, impossibly large shipyard cranes, how they appear to be holding their heads in mourning. George turns to me, "He didn't leave instructions about this? I wanted to be sure. I mean … yes, the water, of course. But here?"

I look away. "No, he didn't leave any instructions at all." Two seagulls land on the railing, their feathers ruffle in the wind. One starts screeching, a high-pitched repetitive scream.

This is when Neil starts laughing. Not a real laugh at all. A kind of humph that he draws out again and again. "No instructions. No way. That John sure didn't leave instructions."

"Please," I say.

"Please what?"

"We just wondered about going out with the *Ginz* as well," Lisa says, her eyes jumping from me to Neil. "Maybe we should save some ashes for somewhere else, too. Up near the islands, maybe."

"I mean it," I say to Neil. "You've missed the point."

Neil stops laughing and holds himself very still. "This isn't about a point."

"You have to understand …"

"No," he shouts, and I realize he's still holding my dad's ashes as his arm goes up into the air in his angry gesture. But he keeps his grip, his arm comes down. "No, Ella. *You* have to understand. You cannot make this decision alone."

"God, Neil, she forgot who we were!"

He waves a hand across my statement while Lisa and George step away. "I could injure myself tomorrow. You could get cancer next year. A child can get lost. Or hurt. Or whatever."

Lisa is gathering herself to intervene. I can see it. She's reaching a hand out, but Neil is backing away. Into the rain, toward the railing of the ferry.

"All you've been talking about is fear. And I'm tired of your fear. You are not your mother. You are not sick."

George cuts in, "Ella? How can we help?"

"It isn't anyone's business," I say. The rain is pelting down my face.

"It's my business!" Neil yells. "Can't you get that into your head? It's my business!"

People inside the ferry are staring at us now. We are almost at the Vashon pier. The boat will slow down and dock.

"Neil," George says. "Ella."

Lisa opens her arms to us, says, "We can talk about this."

Neil throws his arms up again. He's forgotten about the ashes. All I can do is watch his arms. Little plumes of soot are starting to escape from the box.

"Neil!"

"And what?" he yells. "Do you want my permission? Oh yes, Ella. Go ahead. Of course I'll give you my permission."

He tries to cross his arms, but cannot complete the movement. The box stops him. Ashes spill down the front of his coat.

Behind him is the tip of Blake Island. The rain is still so heavy. It's washing the ashes from him almost immediately. A thin trail of soot streaks its way down his coat, puddles at his feet.

"Look what you're doing!" I shout at him, reach for the box.

But he steps away. "Don't touch me, I don't want you to touch me."

"The ashes," Lisa says. "Darling!"

He raises the box high and shakes his head. "Anyway, you've made it clear I am not to be a part of this decision."

"Just give me those," I say, crying now. My entire body taut with the force of my crying.

But he doesn't, he's still holding them. The box is half-open now, and the wind is picking up more ashes, spilling them out. The water catches them right away. My dad is washing out onto the deck of the ferry.

George is yelling now, trying to get the box from Neil. But Neil can't seem to come back to us, he's still shouting. I reach for him too but it's no use, he's all tight limbs and hard energy. I lose sight of the box in his movements, slip on the wet deck and nearly fall. I catch myself and when I look up, I see Lisa place a hand over her eyes. She yells, "Oh my God!"

For a moment I think Neil must have jumped. That he's gone over the side of the boat and this is why Lisa has averted her face. But it isn't that.

George's face is all black, streaked with water. That's when I feel it, the sooty grit on my cheek. And a plume hits Lisa, a thin one, mixes with the rain and slides down like a black tear toward her chin. I touch my own face, my fingers come back to me black and gritty.

Neil is holding the ripped box in his hands and the ashes are everywhere. I see his face, I see it flash—he's shocked, he's ashamed. But he wipes his hands against his windbreaker and the line of his jaw tightens in this movement. "There," he says. "That's done, then. Goodbye, John. Now we can go."

George is watching him, stunned, white lipped.

But then Neil shakes his head and says, "No, actually, it's fine, Ella. You do what you have to do. But that is it for me." He tosses the ripped box into the water—gently at least, he tosses it with a certain carefulness. He shakes his hands, he backs away. He slips on the rain though and grips the door handle back into the inside deck to right himself. His hand on the handle is still covered in ashes. His shoes, too. He's gone gray.

Lisa is holding a hand to her mouth. George is shaking his head, eyes wide. The water below the ferry glistens black. George and Lisa and I stand at the railing. She holds onto me and I don't know who's shaking the hardest. But I blink back the rain and my tears and wipe at my wet face. The rain has taken most of the ashes by now. I'm left with red wind-chapped hands that I must rub and rub in the pouring rain, to clean the remaining ashes from my fingernails and knuckles, while the ocean froths and churns against the side of the boat.

29

IT TAKES ME JUST UNDER FIVE HOURS to spot the first sign. *Friends' Farm, 3 miles.* I've left the highway some time ago and have been winding along smaller farm roads. Driving slowly. This sign means I put my foot on the brakes and pull over. A tractor lumbers its way around me, the farmer looking with vague irritation down into my car. Which is a mess: Daisie and Trapp in the back, coffee cups and granola bar wrappers on the floor. A print out of the directions. My purse, my phone, a packet of chewing gum on the seat beside me.

I don't know why I've stopped. Just to think. Or not to think. Where I've left, where I'm going. I close my eyes against all of it— Neil's soot-covered shoes backing away, the box in the water, Lisa asking me again and again about the argument. I've pushed the brake pedal so hard my leg is trembling where the muscle seizes; I lift it and get going again. The car creeps along for another mile and a half. George and Lisa drove me home after the ferry, refusing to let me stay alone. Lisa sat beside me and stared hard at my face when I insisted I would go to my appointment, then she insisted she come with me. "You will not do this alone. I want to be with you no matter what you decide." I let her come, and she put a hand on my shoulder when I signed the forms and made my real appointment for two days time.

Neil didn't call or come back to my dad's. I keep telling myself that this is what had to happen.

I also keep telling myself that I've driven to Oregon for purely legal reasons. Her name on the deed, the fact of her not knowing about my dad's accident. It's my responsibility, I remind myself, biting back the anger, the confusion. Just a task I need to accomplish and get over.

I pass several farms and country houses and this time a turn is indicated. *Friends' Farm: a cooperative collective.* I pull over just past this sign. The dogs are fidgeting. Their noses have covered the back window with snot and fogged up the glass.

"Settle," I tell them.

I wedge the car alongside a wooden fence and I let the dogs out into a nearby field. Watch them race and circle. Their heads lowered, their noses busy reading the land—the mouse tunnels, the mole hills, the rocks and clumps of weeds. I love seeing Daisie so focused, her entire body taut with a task. Her bird-dog instincts. Trapp is more concerned with me, always racing forward and racing back to check if I've moved. I breathe and breathe and watch them. It's really cold this afternoon but here in Oregon, farther from the sea, there is always less fog, less rain. The winter sun is already waning, but it holds off to the west above us like a ball of bright cold fire. I pull my wool hat down over my ears, wrap my scarf more tightly. There are other things in the car—the boxes and gifts and cards. Her signature. The paperwork for the cabin. I am here and I will have to keep going.

Before I left this morning I tried to send a text to Neil anyway: *I've found her. In Oregon. Going today.*

But I deleted it before sending and I've turned off my phone. The last image flickered as the phone went off, my home screen—a snowy owl in flight, arms spread wide. Silent. Hunting.

I whistle for the dogs, hustle them back into the car, and continue on. Just a short distance from this field the road narrows, turns into more of a gravel track. The trees are taller here, casting a shadow, and then I find myself stopped before a kind of gate. *Friends' Farm* is handwritten on a wooden sign. *Drive straight for General Store*, on another sign beside it. Alongside the gate is a security camera and I don't look into the lens. I cannot tell if it is even on. I get out and open the gate and then scurry back into the car.

I am barely pressing on the accelerator, just letting the car roll forward of its own momentum. These are the gates to my mother's country and I am expecting a stronger boundary than simple wood and trees. A checkpoint would be nicer. With border guards and bomb sniffing dogs. Someone who will listen to the excuses for my intrusion, who will understand that I'm not really here because I want to be. This humble little road makes me uneasy.

I pass a farm stand, but it's all boarded up. Next to the stand is a sign with an arrow pointing toward a small road and the spray painted words, *winter preserve market*. I pass this and then before I can stop and reverse, before I back myself out and off this road, I find I have arrived in front of an A-frame cabin and there is a group of people standing outside of it. Men and women, dressed in flannel shirts and wool sweaters, dark knitted hats and gloves, in jeans and work boots.

I stop the car, lean across the seat and roll down the passenger side window. I am looking, but keeping my head tucked. My lips grow cold, my mouth is dry. Wind hits my face. She isn't one of them. She isn't one of them.

"You here for the preserves?" a woman asks, leaning down. Her hair is long and blonde, like a teenager would wear, but by her face I put her in her early fifties. She's holding a steaming mug of hot liquid in a hand covered in fingerless gloves. "We still have a few. Some good ones."

"I'm not here for preserves," I say, still searching their faces. She isn't here.

"The General Store opens again at two," a man with round spectacles offers. "If you go up another half-mile you'll see it."

"I'm looking for someone," I say, my voice catching. "I'm trying to find someone."

The blonde woman steps closer to the car, leans all the way into the open window. She checks the car, not me. "You've lost someone?"

I am silenced by this. She is still looking around the car. At the animals and the mess. "Are you on vacation? Did you lose someone at the rest area?" Her brow is furrowed now, her eyes dancing from seat to seat.

A man in a bright purple sweater and a full beard repeats her question but with greater distress. "She lost one of her kids at the Whittaker Creek rest area?"

A buzz rises from this small group and they move together into a knot. A woman with thick glasses and a moon face peers into the car.

"No, no," I say, opening the door and half-standing. Looking at them all. "I haven't lost … I said … I'm looking for someone." The dogs are restless, pushing at each other to get out.

I cross around the hood of the car to meet the blonde woman, remove my hat and hold out my hand to say, "I'm … I'm looking for Maggie Tomlinson. Do you know where I might find her?"

The man with spectacles smiles. "Oh, sure." His eyes scan my face and light up with the joy of recognition. Brace yourself, I think, you have heard this before. But instead, he smiles again and says, "You must be Ella."

With this, I am enveloped into the great mass of them, become the center of their words and outstretched arms, of the scent of patchouli and flannel, fleece and wool. Everyone is saying how happy they are to finally meet me. Everyone wants to shake my hand. They're all too close. I try to step backward but the man in the purple sweater is behind me, smiling shyly. I shuffle to the right, shuffle to the left, try to find an exit.

The blonde woman steps in front of me. "I'm Greta."

I shake her hand, although I think I've shaken it already twice.

"So …" she says.

"So …" I say.

"You got the herb and vegetable tags?"

"I'm sorry?"

"Those were mine. I mean, I make them to sell at the stands." When I say nothing, she shrugs, "Oh, it's no matter. It's not the time. Did you have a long drive?"

What can I say? "It isn't so long."

I swallow, I breathe. I reach for one of the dogs with the flat of my hand. Trapp's small round forehead presses back against my palm and I am able to say, "So you all know Maggie? This is where she lives?"

A general muttering of agreement rises up. They flick a few glances back and forth from one another. Maybe I'm supposed to know this already.

Press, press, press against Trapp's head. Feel the soft of his fur. "Can someone tell me where to find her? Or let her know that I'm here."

A kind of silence rolls out from their five faces. They look at one another, they shift in their stances.

The man with the beard says, "You drove down by yourself? Caroline or Neil couldn't come with you?"

Caroline? I shake my head, utterly confused.

He says, "Oh, that's too bad. I hope it was okay coming on your own. Maggie wouldn't have liked that."

But the moon-faced woman interrupts, "Maggie's not here today. She's away on farm business." Her face is dry, her lips very chapped.

Greta smiles. "But she'd want us to ask you to stay and wait for her."

So I know we're talking about the wrong Maggie. That all of this has been some kind of mistake. There must be another woman who looks just like me.

But those five faces are all nodding at me, in unison. Smiling at this idea and agreeing with one another. The man with round spectacles takes off his hat; his hair is bright red underneath. He says, "You'll stay won't you? She'll be back tomorrow. We have a guest cabin. You can stay one night, right?" His eyes are so solemn. Too solemn. I remember the same mixture of steady concentration and vague emotion in the expressions of the men's faces at the 23rd Street Project.

I can't stay, I think. Of course I can't stay. But my mother has been living here at *Friends' Farm* for nearly ten years; she's managed to create a home for herself here and I think—the thought rises up like a physical sensation—I think I deserve to know what After really looks like. I agree to stay.

Two of them clap their hands and Greta says, "Wonderful! Now let's all go back to the store and introduce ourselves properly."

This is what I learn: the commune is composed of ten members, seven of whom I meet right away out on that road and in the General Store, more women than men, and they range in age from thirties to sixties, although Maggie is clearly one of the eldest.

Greta tells me that Maggie and another woman, Anna, are off attending a winter farmer's market.

"We do this year-round, and all over the country really. We have stalls and buyers up and down the coast."

Tom, the red-haired man, says, "Our farthest customer is in Maine, but they order jams and honeys and we can just ship that stuff."

"Anyway," Greta continues, "This week was Maggie's turn. She was in Idaho and Washington last week, California now. So that's the way the cookie crumbles." She laughs and two others laugh with her.

I watch the bearded man, whose name is Hal, lead Trapp by the collar through the rows of homemade candies. There is peanut brittle and caramel and salt water taffy. Trapp is sniffing it all, nosing his way but not daring to actually lick or steal anything. The man gets him to a bin and pulls out what looks like a dog biscuit. Daisie is being caressed by multiple hands and is quivering with bliss, her eyes halfway closed, ears laid down.

We are inside a large A-frame building, in a room separated into two halves. On this half is the store, with large wooden shelves lined with goods. The gourd utensils are here. The sachets of potpourri, those unmistakable jam jars. Beeswax candles and homemade soaps. All the odd objects and goods I found in the cabin. I observe and comment and admire because this is what seems to be expected of me. There are knitted hats and scarves and even sweaters. Cloth wall hangings and table runners.

"Elizabeth is our weaver," Greta explains, pointing at the woman with thick glasses and birthmark. "William is the woodworker." She indicates a tall black man standing behind the check-out counter. He gives me a short nod.

"And yourself?"

"I'm the gardener," she says. "I make all the planting and harvesting decisions. Except for the Christmas trees. That's William's territory. I should have said he's an arborist *and* a woodworker."

"Everyone has a specific job?"

"That's how we work. Without that as our foundation we would crumble as a community. We have some students who help us, especially in the summers when there is so much land work to do."

She tells me before I ask that Maggie is their accountant. "She takes care of all the money. But she's also my second hand at planting and gardening decisions. She has quite the green thumb!"

Beyond the General Store, the other half of the room is clearly a dining area. Tables and chairs and coffee pots on a side bar, and carafes for water or juice. A bookshelf fills an entire wall, paperbacks lined up along each row, magazines stacked in piles. Near the door which seems to lead into a kitchen is a large green chalkboard. The days of the week are laid out with various chores: breakfast, lunch, dinner, dishes, garbage and so forth. Next to the tasks are the names, changing for each day. I can see that on Monday Maggie made breakfast.

People mill over from the store to the dining room and begin to sit in the chairs and around the tables. I am asked to take a seat at a round table between Anna and Tom. The dogs follow me and Daisie, who has had enough attention from strangers, sits at my feet, presses her shoulder against my knee.

"We didn't plan anything special for supper," Tom explains. "We didn't know we'd have a guest."

"You don't need to do anything special for me."

A man, whose name I later learn is Isaac, approaches and points to Daisie. "These are your animals. That's what Hal said. I take care of the animals here at the farm." His speech is monotone and his eyes unblinking.

I tell him that yes, I'm a veterinarian. "And what animals do you have?"

"We have chickens. We have goats. We have cats. No one has a dog, but if someone wanted to, we have agreed to say yes."

I try to think of something else to say, but nothing comes. Eventually Isaac nods at me and says, "Being a vet is a good job. I'm glad to hear you're a vet." Then he walks away.

Elizabeth leans in, "Issac works very hard to communicate efficiently."

Tom nods. "He doesn't always know what to say. But he tries really hard."

I accept a pre-supper mug of cinnamon tea. Ask more questions about everyone's role. Elizabeth proves to be a great source of information. She is so relaxed it is difficult for me to decide what her illness might be. Because everyone here most certainly has an illness. This is what brings them together. There is no grandiose social living construct, no socialist ideals except those necessitated by the eccentricities of their disorders. A new experiment, Erica Reza called it. It seems to be working.

Across the table during the meal sits a woman named Lilah. Greta introduced her to me when I first came in but she hurried off to finish cooking the evening meal and only returned a few moments ago. She is a tiny creature, and clearly the youngest here. She might even be younger than me. Her cheekbones look painful, her lips are stretched and too red, and her wrists so thin I fear they will break if she lands one too hard against the wooden tabletop. When she came out of the kitchen carrying a huge cauldron of soup, I'd nearly rushed over to help her. And then she'd spent a long time arranging it on the table, pushing and fussing over it and setting out napkins into three perfect stacks beside it.

Eventually, she sat down, tapped her hands five times, palms down on the wood, and finally started eating. Some of the members bowed their heads in prayer, others didn't, but they waited for the prayers to finish. Not Lilah. She started eating, breaking bread into hunks and dipping it into her soup and then taking long drinks from a tall glass of milk next to her plate.

I watch her. She alternates soup with milk, never once taking two gulps of milk or two spoonfuls of soup. She speaks to no one and no one speaks to her. When her bowl and glass are empty, she stands up and carries them into the kitchen.

Elizabeth and Tom are telling me about their plans for renting out some of the beehives later in the spring, about the need to keep the local orchards well pollinated. I nod and listen and when Isaac, seated next to Tom, leans in to ask questions about the veterinary needs of honeybees, I must focus completely on him. His direct gaze requires this. So it is a shock when Lilah appears beside me and moves in between Elizabeth and myself; she leans down, her face close to mine. There are violet semi-circles, like bruises, below her eyes.

"If you want to talk about your mother, come outside. I'm going to smoke."

Everyone has played my game. I called my mother Maggie and they called her Maggie to me. Despite everyone knowing odd things about me like where I work, where I live and the name of my pets, they have mostly behaved like I am just some disinterested visitor, someone here to see about selling land to the commune or retailing their products.

I excuse myself so quickly the dogs must leap out of the way as my chair screeches across the polished floor. Lilah moves with little steps, rotating her feet outward. Elegant but a little choppy, and I feel oversized and clumsy, the way I always feel around small women.

Outside we sit on a verandah. Benches with rounded backs and lumpy cushions. The air is harsh and cold, but smells fresh. A pile of blankets awaits and Lilah takes the first one and throws it over her head. There is a slit cut out of the middle and arm holes. She hands me another one and I sit and put it over my lap like a normal blanket. She is sitting cross-legged on the bench and arranges the blanket around her like a teepee.

"Can I ask you something?" she says, pulling a long thin cigarette from somewhere inside her teepee.

I nod. But she doesn't ask anything right away and I wonder whether she has seen my head move in the dim light. Beyond the small porch it is pitch black, and only a small lamp above our heads casts a weak yellow light. There are no insects in this cold December air, only the crisp dark line of trees across the road. "Ask away," I say, hoping to sound relaxed.

"What are you, two, three months along?"

"I'm sorry?"

"I'm not clairvoyant, don't worry," she says, sniggering and standing abruptly. She reaches out to the railing and slaps the wood. Once with her right hand and once with her left, her cigarette stuck between her lips. She sits back down. "I'm not hiding here to keep a secret like that from the rest of the world. And I'm not crazy either." Here she gives me a stern glance. "I'm just really good at guessing things like this."

"How can you tell?"

"I just can. It's a body thing. The body moves differently when you're pregnant." I feel her look at me, although I do not return the glance. "You did know you were pregnant, right?"

"I am only barely."

She smiles. "Good. I once spilled the beans to someone in serious denial." She stands and performs her slapping gesture on the railing.

"You had something to tell me about Maggie?"

She sits back down again and inhales from her cigarette. "I like Maggie. She's got her head on right." A pause. A short laugh. "For someone with delusions."

I shift in my seat.

"Sorry," she says. She does not sound sorry. "I only talk like this because I'm jealous. My therapist tells me this. Let me repeat something for you: I am jealous of people with incurable disorders." She rubs her cigarette out into a coffee can filled with sand. Reaches for another. "It's like this," she says, holding the thin cigarette up for me to inspect. "Beautiful, isn't it?"

"It's a cigarette."

"I'm talking about the aesthetic. A perfect form. Elegant."

"Not very sturdy though," I say.

"Don't I know it?"

I am shivering now, but in sympathy. I hope she's getting the right kind of help. But I am thankful too because my patients cannot do this, my animals are mute and usually fixable.

After lighting her second cigarette, Lilah squints at me, "I have something to tell you, but I have another question first."

"I'm not sure I can answer your questions."

"It isn't a hard one this time. And maybe it won't be a surprise."

"Did you know about this place?" She stands and slaps the railing. "Did you know about Maggie living here?"

I reach a hand for that railing but retract it before making contact. I consider telling her the truth, that I thought my mother was missing or dead, that I was sure she was safely wrecked and rotting deep beneath the ocean of my life. How I preferred this story to any other, no matter how many times it was proven wrong. But I say nothing, staring out at the night. The darkness beyond this bench is so complete my eyes don't know what to do with it. They just stretch and stare and hope. But nothing takes shape. Nothing is defined.

Lilah answers for me. "I didn't think so. Some of us have wondered."

"But everyone seems to know me."

She nods. "We have to believe one another here. That's part of the deal."

I look at her. Everyone has their trades.

"So how did you find out?" There is a pause. "I guess that makes two questions. Sorry." She stands and slaps the railing again.

"My dad died," I say. Three simple words. A possessive, a noun, and a verb. Is there another way I might move those words around and come up with an acceptable phrase?

"Did you know your dad?"

I cannot answer right away and Lilah takes this for something else. "My dad wasn't around much either. His money was, but not him."

"No," I say, and there is violence in my voice. "My dad was around."

Lilah waits a moment. Then, "Lucky you." After a pause, she says, "Some of us met your dad, he came once or twice. But Maggie never said when, never invited him to eat with us."

Lilah is on her third cigarette and all this furious smoking is starting to annoy me. She holds up the cigarette, "The skinny ones don't last long, do they?"

"That's one way of putting it."

"At least I'm not throwing up anymore." Her voice has grown small. "Stains the teeth. Not a pretty sight. And very hard to hide, even in footlights." Here she stands again, letting the blanket fall around her bony frame. She raises her arms and then one leg; it rises with a gentle curve, flicks and swivels behind her, when it comes down she rises on her toes. But her supporting leg trembles and she bring the other one down quickly. She slaps the railing again, first right and then left. Lifts her cigarette to her mouth and draws hard.

"So what did you want to tell me?" I ask, resisting the urge to wave the smoke away from my face.

She pulls deep on her cigarette, breathes the smoke out. "Maggie writes everything down. Everything."

"And?"

"And she keeps it in her cabin. Everything she writes down."

"How long have you known her?" I am thinking about trust. About how this community works, and I'm guessing that Lilah won't last very long here. But it isn't my business.

"Four years. Nearly four years. That's how long I've been here. It's not easy, this communal living thing. Maggie's one of the founders. She's got insight."

I shake my head. This is too much. My mother knows nothing of communal living.

Lilah sits back down inside her teepee. "So were your parents still together? Or what? Maggie explained about a cabin up in Washington, on the ocean, that we could use if we needed a break from the commune."

"He leant it to her?"

"A few of us have gone. For a day or two. Always alone. But I wondered if when she went, your dad was there, too. That's another thing I've never figured out."

Maybe they were together in a way that I won't be able to understand. And certainly not Lilah. I shrug and toss out, "It's complicated."

"Things are never as complicated as you think they are. We learn that on day one."

I don't try to disagree with her.

She laughs, just to herself. But she doesn't speak. She isn't with me anymore. She's with her own story. I watch her for a moment, then I say, "I'll go back inside."

She snaps to me, though, watching me for a moment, holding my gaze. Lilah's hands are twittering around inside her teepee for another cigarette. "It isn't her fault, you know. It's a disease. You should learn this. You wouldn't blame someone for being hurt in a car accident, would you? Think of it like that. It happened to her."

Lilah's sentence is interrupted by the hooting of an owl off in the forest beyond the building. Long and low, it echoes throughout the night.

We listen to it. Both of us. Then I say, "Well, no, actually, car accidents make me pretty angry, too."

30

WHEN EVERYONE IS FINISHED EATING, Greta walks me to the guest cabin. The path is soft with a thick layer of needles. The night sky has become the deepest velvet black and the only light comes from a series of small lamps belted to some of the trees. Greta gives me softly mumbled indications—"There's a thick root here, watch your step," and "It forks here, we'll go right." A line of cedars hedge us in, their boughs heavy in the cold air. I picture the branch of cedar pine cones, like geese in flight, that Neil gave me several days ago and the imaginary feel of it in my hand causes a dull ache to spread across my chest. Such gifts. And I've refused them. I shut the thought down. The dogs are ecstatic to be outside again. They switchback from left to right, noses to the ground, darting off the path, darting back around my feet. Then I leash Daisie who is more prone to run off after the sound or scent of a wild animal.

"Will the other one stay with you?" Greta asks. "Here we turn left."

"He's not a hunter at all. He just wants to shepherd everything. Mostly me."

She nods. Smiles. Then points down a branching path. "That way to our cabins, most of them."

"How long have you lived here?" I ask.

"I came after my daughter died. Six years ago now."

Like an electrical storm rising up on a vast plain, a surge of anger whips through me. Have all these people here left people behind. What about Greta's husband or other children?

"You moved here because you lost a daughter?"

"In a way, yes. Tom and I needed a quiet space."

My storm quiets, calms. "Tom is your husband?"

"He's always struggled with his anxiety, but after Sage died ..." She raises her head and looks up. "Losing your child is a backward kind of thing. It turns everything inside out and upside down."

"I'm sorry," I say.

The path narrows and I step behind Greta. We reach a fork and Greta indicates to the right, "Those are the rest of our cabins." I can see a few porch lights, the vague outline of small windows, but the night is very dark. Very cold. She walks to the left and says, "But we have three guest cabins this way. It isn't far." A minute or so later the path opens up onto a clearing which houses three small A-frame cabins. As we walk up the steps of the first, Greta sniffs the air. "It smells like snow."

I sniff. The air is dry and cold. "It smells clean."

"Snow is clean. You should be warm enough, but add more wood before you sleep if you'd like."

The cabin is painted green and yellow. A wreath of dried flowers decorates the front door. Greta unlocks this and then hands me the key. Inside there are three single beds. A sink in the corner and a small bathroom. There is not much space to move around in, but it's neat and cozy. Warm from the wood stove already burning. I place my bag on the floor near the fire. The beds are laid with thick quilts.

"Elizabeth's handiwork?"

Greta smiles. "No, Anna. Anna is our quilter. You'll meet her tomorrow when she and Maggie return."

Maggie. My mother.

The dogs sniff the room from corner to corner and then tramp down a small piece of carpet in front of the stove and curl up. Like a magician, Greta produces two twists of jerky from her pocket and places it in front of each of them before saying goodnight and closing the door behind her.

I am not even a little bit sleepy and so I sit on the floor with the animals, listening to their thick breathing and feeling the heat that radiates from their warm bodies. Daisie shifts her head onto my leg. I watch them, losing myself in the color gradations of their fur, the slow expansion and flattening of their flanks, the gentle twitching of their limbs in sleep. It comes to me that Neil has given me Trapp without any discussion. It also comes to me that I assumed the dog was mine. I have behaved all along as though there was no question of sharing. The ache in my chest returns, the weight of what I've decided. What I have to do.

After the clinic, Lisa argued both for and against my decision like a true feminist, while George shook his head and cried for me and Neil. Both of them hugged me. And both of them insisted I drive to *Friends' Farm* and see my mother.

"Think of it like that," Lilah said. "It happened to her."

No, I think, it happened to us. It happened to me. And in two seconds I am up and out the door, heading toward the commune member cabins.

It's very dark now, a deep fog blocking the tiny lights along the path. I crunch across the pine needles, finger the rough bark of the trees, and send pine cones sliding with my tennis shoes as I stumble along, half-blind. Trapp keeps just in front of me, and every so often he slides back next to my hip to have his ears petted but then he slinks ahead again. Daisie, leashed, pads softly behind.

We reach a first clearing with a staggering of several cabins. One of the cabin lights turns off as I approach; two remain lit. At first I sit on a bench, waiting, looking. But a nervous energy makes this impossible, so I stand and walk the path back to the other set of member cabins. Even the dogs seem to understand the importance of this silent mission and walk carefully, quietly. I can hear the rush of a river somewhere, the churning crash of a waterfall in the forest beyond the commune. Or maybe this is the sound of the blood in my ears, the race in my heart. But then it's snowing. As if the fog has crystallized and burst into flakes. Almost instantly I can see again. The moonlight reflects through the white as it falls, as it lands on my arms and legs and shoes, as it begins to coat the trees and gild the backs of the dogs. The more it snows, the more I can see.

Back and forth I walk along, passing the cabins, passing through the forest along the twisty paths. It isn't too long before all the cabin lights are out. In the first clearing, a man's snoring reaches me. I picture each of the commune members in sleep, faces relaxed, mouths slack. I wonder if their dreams are as organized or as stressful as their days. I wonder if they are haunted by their former lives, by the people they have left behind or the people that have been left by. I wonder if Lilah still dances in her sleep, if Greta dreams of her lost child.

I brush the snow from my arms and face and move more deliberately now, not hovering at the edge of the clearings but walking along to see the fronts of the now-dark cabins. It is snowing so hard now, my feet leave impressions.

These cabins are considerably larger than the guest cabin. Two-room structures, but sizable for a single person. There are four in a cluster, four in another, and another two off aways down a third path—and for the first time I wonder how the commune came to be, who designed it, did the founding members of *Friends' Farm* build it themselves, or did they purchase it. Each cabin has a slender front porch jutting off from its symmetrical double windows and centered door. The decorations vary: flowers, birdhouses, a potted tree, carved signs. On one porch sits a statue of the Hindu god Ganesh.

How will I do this, I wonder, worrying how to determine whose cabin is whose. I walk slowly. Quietly. Looking at each porch and door. Up one path, into a clearing, back toward the other clearing. I assume the cabins without flower boxes or with very little decoration belong to the men. But this is proven wrong when I see nameplates on two of the doors—William on one, beside a mini Christmas tree, still decorated, and Elizabeth on the other. I pass a cabin with light blue curtains. I decide that my mission is not only dishonest, but impossible. I turn around, ready to leave the second clearing and go back to sleep, but then am stopped by a painted sculpture sitting on the railing of the third cabin. I move closer. A bit more, and then tilt. Because here is Lizzy. The same wing-like fins, bright scales and white patches. The same flat-nosed face. Only this Lizzy is much larger than the original ever was, the size of a goldfish bowl, whereas the real Lizzy had been small enough to fit in the cup of my ten-year-old hands.

The other three cabins in this clearing are totally dark. I step onto that little porch and put my hand on Lizzy's cold dorsal fin. The statue is made from rough-grained clay and even though it is painted I can feel the hardened granules under my fingertips. I sweep my fingers back and forth, pressing harder and pushing at the cold hard surface. The fish's mouth is open, a perfect O. It is being used as a vase, and a thin pine bough stands at attention from between its red lips. I remove the branch.

I put my free hand on the front door of the cabin. It is not locked.

This simple testament to how safe my mother feels living at the commune nearly stops me from entering. I think to leave the truth of her safety intact.

But I am not yet ready for this trade and so I open the door anyway. It's dark at first but I wait and my eyes adjust to the brightness from the snow-filtered moonlight. It's enough and I start to make-out the shapes and forms in the room. A bed, a wardrobe, a lamp. A rug across the floor, a desk along the wall. It doesn't take me long to see that Lizzy is also inside the cabin. A small fish hanging on the wall above the window. Another sculpture, smaller than the porch railing one, sits atop a dresser near the far wall. I cross the room and pick up the fish on the dresser.

I put the fish back in its exact spot between a photo of my dad in his yellow rain slicker and a bouquet of dried roses tied with a purple string.

But it isn't just the fish. I'm there in that cabin, too. Stapled to a bulletin board are photographs of me as a child. Of my dad, too. On his ferry. On the beach in his fishing gear. Near the closet is a small watercolor of my seven- or eight-year-old face. In a frame near a small sofa is a photo of my college graduation. Another of my dad, wearing a baseball cap and smiling. And then one of Neil's and my wedding. And there are the mirrors. Three or four of them so that every which way that I turn, I can see my adult face. I can see her. Everywhere. Ella and Maggie. Maggie and Ella.

I examine these photographs, finger the edge of her bedspread, put my hands into a pair of gloves on a small table by the door. I open her closet and touch her clothes. I breathe deep because I do not remember what she smelled like. Did she smell like this? I recognize none of these clothes. I step inside. I reach my hand inside the sleeve of a sweater. I breathe deep because I don't know anything about this woman. Turning back to the room I search for a shelf, or a desk. She writes everything down, Lilah told me. But of course I already know this.

"Look," she always said, pencil in hand, scribbling notes while I would try to follow the rise and fall of her pencil. Arm out, finger extended. Then back to the paper. Lists and phrases and letters.

"Look," I whisper.

And I do. The desk against the far wall is a narrow rectangle of soft old wood. It looks old but not used. It is fairly neatly organized: a ceramic vase filled with pencils and pens, a photo of the ocean (I recognize it as the twin of the photo in Erica Reza's office hallway), a small plastic tray with paperwork, a candy tin with no lid filled with paperclips and a pencil sharpener. Beside the desk is a narrow bookshelf, more like a shelf for holding CDs. And this is filled with notebooks. I sit at her desk. I place my hands on the wood where she would place her hands. I imagine they are the same size. I reach for a notebook at random. Place it before me and shift just enough to get the moonlight. It's still snowing outside. The circle of grass between the cabins is growing white, brighter.

The pages are all very similar, filled with what looks like lists. Almost a kind of ledger. With dates and descriptions of … it's hard to understand just what … activities? names? objects? The notebook I've chosen includes dates from 2012:

> 3/16/2012—*Michael F. Canstoni, 47 years old, University of Michigan*
>
> 3/18/2012—*Animal Behavior Meets Microbial Ecology* (this item has a check mark beside it in red ink)
>
> 3/25/2012—*McGraw St., 2:33pm, red cars, safe*
>
> 4/16/2012—*Freestead Coffee Co, blonde*
>
> 7/24/2012—*726, and 12, safe*

The list goes on and on. I scan it, not understanding, pulling my scarf closer around my neck. Switch to another notebook. This one is for 2014:

11/26/2014—Mr. and Mrs., Labrador, 8:23am, safe
12/2/2014—crampons, two wool hats
12/2/2014—Madison, Wilson, Jefferson

I search back through the stack, squinting to decipher some of her handwriting in the dim light. The oldest notebooks are from late 2005. She was living at the 23rd Street Project by then. It strikes me that these are a kind of diary. I could sit and read them and try to work out who she was, what she was doing, where she was.

"You remember how she was," my dad is saying. "How she always noticed things. Your mom had the wildest imagination."

I flip through the notebooks and begin to work out who she was, what she was doing.

8/29/2009—small apartment, Pullman (J: safe)
8/30/2009—Veterinary Cell Physiology I

My fingertip stops mid-trace. Re-traces the line from the beginning. I place the book slowly onto the table, look again into the first one I pulled out. *Michael Canstoni.* And then *McGraw Street*, in Seattle. Back to this one from 2009. My finger moving down the page. This isn't really her diary. Michael Canstoni was one of the associate vets I interned for in 2012. He was only in the office a few weeks and then moved on. But there he is. Documented. A part of my life.

I have no idea about the journal article mentioned below his name, but this kind of listing is everywhere through her notebooks. Article and book titles in veterinary science. Tucked into the notebooks are newspaper clippings as well—The Seattle P.I., the Seattle Times, the WSU Daily Evergreen, even The Wenatchee World. The dates correspond to the years I have lived in these different cities. Many of the clippings are highlighted, written upon. What is highlighted are crimes or violent events. A news item about a street brawl includes this in her handwriting: *20–30% chance.* An article about hazing on Washington State University campus includes this: *4/17/2009—safe.* This word repeated everywhere. *Safe. Safe. Safe.* In a few places it's written, *(J: safe).* Is J my dad? Are we both safe? Did he tell her I was safe? And so many dates and streets and events. *Safe.* I unwind my scarf, wind it right back up. It is nearly eleven p.m. It is still snowing outside the window. Snowing hard now. The moonlight is white, crisp.

I start from the beginning, reading through each notebook from first page to last page. I find it all. My marriage and my degrees. My cities. My work colleagues. Caroline is listed and so is Alex, the consulting vet. Everyone. She has checked everyone. It takes me a long long time and when I pluck out and open the last notebook on the shelf, which finishes in June of last summer, I can hardly see a thing she has written. It doesn't matter. It will all be about me.

How easily the world splits. How simple it is to get everything wrong. I thought I'd worked out long ago who was the villain and who was the hero. And yet both of them were protecting me, however best they could. My dad could never have allowed this woman back into my life. She might have suffocated me, suffocated us both. Too much love, how does that even work? This is a trade I could never have expected. The cabin is fully dark now, the moon gone, the snow outside the window no longer illuminated but shadowy and cold. Gathering in drifts. The flurries have become a full-fledged storm. I return the notebook to its shelf. Sit again with my hands on the wood where she might place her hands. I steal one of her pencils, tuck it into the pocket of my coat. I look at the desk, at the neatness of it. The alignment of the notebooks. Her clothes hanging in the closet. Her made bed, and carefully arranged pillow.

Delusional disorder: the great muddy flood of my mother, the messiest room of my entire life.

31

WHAT REALLY HAPPENED THE DAY my mother left is this.

Yes, I go down to the pier, scour the terminal building, scour the exit, am frightened by the one-legged man and I run back into the building to call my dad. Only before I get to the telephone, I see her.

She is over by the far exit. In a chair. There are a few other people near her. She has a pencil and a notebook in her hand, and she's taking notes. Furiously. She could be a normal traveler. Someone on her way home from a conference or a visit to a friend's house. But I know better. I know *her*. She's crazy. She's left us and I am so angry I can't take a step toward her.

Still, I watch her and for a moment I imagine she is waiting for me like we are traveling together and I've just run off to the bathroom. I imagine that she might look up and smile at me, reach into her bag and say something like, "Catch if you can," and throw a candy bar at me. She would put her book away and start telling me something fantastic about one of the ferry captains. "He only does this during the day," she could say. "At night he patrols the Puget Sound in a homemade submarine. Except it's shaped like a bus. He wants to create an underwater ferry system, taking passengers from cove to cove."

She's here, so close I can be at her side in just a few steps, can sit next to her because this is what normal mothers and daughters do. And even at ten, I'm aware we look very similar. I've heard our family friends comment on our startling likeness, the way our hair parts in the same place, the way our noses slope at the same angle. We even walk the same. So I know if I sit down even a chair away from her and she doesn't see me, other people will look at us and know she's my mother.

Because she's my mother.

But I don't move. I just keep watching her. Watching her and waiting for the moment when I will know exactly what to do next.

Her head comes up from her notebook and she sees me. I know that she sees me. Her eyes meet mine across the feet that separate us. It is incredible how looking at someone you know can do away with distance. Just erase it. Nothing stands between the fact that I am looking at my mother and she is looking back at me.

I say, "Mom?" although maybe I only whisper it.

"Mommy?"

She's looking at me, and she says, "Hey, look," and she points toward the other side of the room. "I'm taking care of it. You don't have to worry."

I don't look. And she blinks back to her notebook. Writing furiously.

Maybe I could run to her. Grab her arm, shake her and make her look at me. Maybe I could find a policeman or another adult, someone who might help me keep her in one place until my dad can get to us. Maybe this would work. Maybe she will connect back to reality just long enough for the part of her that isn't completely gone to remember, even for just a second.

But I do none of those things. I watch her writing furiously and I revel in my own fury. I stand there hating her. After a few moments, she gets up from her chair and crosses to one of the exits in the direction that she pointed. I don't look to see whether she goes left or right along the street, whether she takes a bus or a taxi. Instead, I envision the line of her back, the narrow of her shoulders as they melt away. I don't imagine her disappearing into a crowd or raising her arm for a taxi. I see myself standing in the small terminal building, the water blue and flat in the windows to the outside, and I don't want to think that's she's just walked away, not just outside, because I prefer to see her walking into the ocean, prefer to see her sinking into the waves, drowning, slipping deeper and deeper to finally settle on the bottom with all the other lost boats. In this way, I create my own secret. When my dad comes to get me I tell him how I failed, how I couldn't find her. But I never tell him that I did see her that day, I never tell him how much I wanted her to go.

32

I wake that second morning at *Friends' Farm* to someone pounding on the cabin door. Pounding hard. Urgent. I sit up in the bed, pulling the quilt up to my chin against the cold that will rush in from outside. Not just against the cold. I am pulling this quilt up like a kind of armor. I am expecting my mother. It seems only right that she might be coming to shoo me away from her home. That she might think I have no right to be here.

But it's Isaac. He's rushed in and hovers in the doorway, breathing hard, the bottom cuffs of his jeans are all wet. Faced flushed, hands trembling. For a man with such controlled expressions, his emotional distress is shouting. His shoulders are hunched, his body tight with the desire for flight.

"Isaac?" I say, sitting up. Snow has come in with him, spilling in from the porch. There is so much snow.

"Help me," he says. "I need your help." There is blood on his sleeve. He reaches for my arm and practically lifts me from the bed, and my instinct is to pull myself away which only frightens him. I am gasping at the cold of the room. He retreats back to the door. I swing my legs from the bed while the dogs jump and race about my feet. I don't even need to ask what has happened because of the way Isaac is staring at the dogs. He's come to find me because I'm a vet. And in a few seconds I'm dressed and pulling my hair into a ponytail. In a few seconds I'm throwing on my coat and following him out the door.

"Tell me," I say. The snow is deep to my knees. Thick and heavy.

"The goats," he says. "The goats are too loud."

"Where are the goats?"

The dogs catch up to me a few steps down the path. The snow is already balling up on Trapp's long fur.

"Where are the goats, Isaac?"

But he's stuttering now, his face tightened down. He's walking fast. "We have eight goats. In four sheds. I built the sheds. They are strong sheds."

"We need my vet bag, Isaac," and I rush as best I can while he follows to where I left my car last night. The car is nearly buried in snow, but Isaac helps me open the trunk without clearing it all, and I grab my supplies. He leads me toward a series of outbuildings beyond the main meeting hall. The sky is still only half-lit, more purple than blue. The snow is so thick on the ground and my running shoes not appropriate at all; my feet are frozen within a few minutes, my jeans stiff and wet. Isaac steps easily in his dark boots, and I try to step where he steps to keep from slipping. I want him to keep talking.

"How long have you had the goats?"

"Two years. I like goats. Good animals."

"Do you make cheese with the goats' milk, or do you sell the milk fresh?"

"Cheese only." He steps over a fallen tree trunk like it's a small stick. "It's easier to store and a more popular product." His voice is clearing, his shoulders less hunched.

"Do they produce a lot of milk?" I ask, scaling the trunk myself.

"About two quarts a day. Very sweet milk."

Now we can hear the goats and Isaac's agitation returns. They are bleating, screaming really, in the way that a hurt goat sounds far too human.

"It will be alright, Isaac. I'm here to help."

He nods at me. "You will know what to do. It's your job." He points a strong flashlight at a small building and I see what has happened. The heavy snow has collapsed the roof and that roof has pushed an inner wall inside the shed.

"I must have miscalculated," Isaac says, his voice choked. "I thought it was sturdy. This is all my fault."

But I'm already running toward the building and trying to get inside. Behind me I hear him say, "I am so angry at myself." But he doesn't sound angry. His words are weighted, but steady. Some commune members are here, too, and they nod at me with their drawn faces. Isaac reaches me and I ask him, "Can you help me, or do you need to stay outside?"

He doesn't answer, he pushes past me to get inside and once we are inside, I see that these are pygmy goats and this is such a relief. Pygmies are calm little creatures and their small size makes them easier to handle.

He gets a light working and then we can see. Several of the goats are quite hurt. One has been killed, her small head crushed beneath a broken piece of wood. I can't even move her out of the way yet. Isaac will help me if I give him clear instructions, and so I ask him to begin work on the roof. Already my hands are running along the scrapes and tears on a young goat's foreleg, but I tell him to clear away as much debris as possible, to make sure the building won't fall in on me or any of the other goats. He stares a moment at the dead doe but then gets to work. He's amazingly fast, ripping back siding and displacing sheets of corrugated metal from what is left of the roof's ceiling. Within minutes the shadowy dawn sky rushes in over my head.

I sort the goats—basic first aid and very hurt. Only one goat seems completely unharmed. William, the woodworker and arborist, comes inside and offers to help. I point him toward the four goats with minor scratches. He works quietly, asking me questions if necessary, and I am grateful for the help.

There are two goats I need to assess. The first goat cannot stand up; her front right leg has been badly injured. Without an x-ray I won't know how much, but I feel around for a fracture and when I do, she lets loose an ear-splitting shriek and shivers in shock. Her lovely eyes roll backward. I rub her eyebrows and her ears. I speak quietly to her, soothing and explaining. William is doing the same in his corner of this half-broken shed. The goats begin to quiet.

I ask William to bring me a tube, any kind of tube and some water. When he does I am able to set the bone, pack the cardboard tube with cotton and wrap the makeshift splint with plaster. I give her something for the pain and within a few minutes she is walking again. She leaves the shed on her own and I can hear the commune members greet her. William has already sent out two of his goats and the situation is improving.

The next goat isn't bleeding or doesn't appear to have broken anything. She can walk but is shivering and rolling her eyes. Flecks of foam have gathered at the corners of her mouth. William finishes cleaning and bandaging his last goat and comes over.

"She's going into labor," he says. "The scare must be too much."

I feel silly for not noticing the goat's side distension. "How far along is she?"

His eyes roll upward, he mouths something. And then, "It's okay, she's due next week."

"Still," I say. "It's going to be a traumatic birth."

He nods and we immediately work to calm the little doe down, talking quietly and gently caressing her nose and ears. But she is still trembling and most likely in pain. If we can get her to calm further, she will probably deliver without any complications—although too quickly, and I'm worried about tearing and blood loss.

"Is this her first kidding?" I ask.

He shakes his head, runs his hand along the spots on her spine. "This will be her third. She knows what to do."

Isaac has gotten the shed nearly completely disassembled, except for a back wall. And now I can see that the entire commune has come out to watch and help. There is Lilah near a fence, cigarette between her fingers. There is Greta with her blonde hair in pigtails and a bandanna on her head, there is Hal and Anna and Isaac moving across in front of them. Their faces are frozen, a little stricken. They remain in a deep silence as they watch what is happening.

William and I sit with the goat, petting and keeping her calm. The other goats, now mostly calm, have gathered where the shed's broken wall used to stand, their rectangular pupils fully dilated in the bright beam of the overhanging lamp. I want to get the dead goat out of the shed as quickly as possible to get their living space back to normal again. But I have learned that it's important the remaining goats stand a moment with the dead goat's body.

William considers the dead animal. "Isaac will take this hard. These are his goats. He's spent the time to raise them and learn how to work with them."

Isaac enters the shed and kneels next to the body of the dead goat. He removes the beam from its head and takes the wood directly outside. He doesn't come back for some time and a few of the other goats approach and stand over the dead goat's body. One goat noses it again and again.

Isaac comes back in with a blanket.

"I can take her?"

I nod, explain that he should leave her, if he likes, outside for a bit. Give all of the goats some access.

Isaac covers the goat's head and scoops the animal up. I can hardly see the small bundle in his large arms. He brings it over to me.

"You see the stripes here," he says, pointing to the goat's flank. "You never know how a Nigerian dwarf will color. You cannot control anything about it, you can't select for spots or stripes or pure tan."

"I didn't know that."

"You have to be prepared for anything. This one was born with miniature spots, all along this left side here. But they turned into stripes as she grew."

I caress the dead goat's flank. "She's lovely."

"And this one," he points to the light tan goat between us, "our ram is pure white, but she gave birth last year to four kids, two perfectly black, one with stripes and one fawn."

I say nothing.

"We're all looking forward to see how the kids will be this year."

He lifts the bundle a little higher in his arms.

"I'm sorry you lost her."

His face is calm now, his body no longer so taut with anxiety. "One day I won't feel sad about it anymore." He walks out, cradling the goat.

Our pregnant goat is beginning to roll her eyes. She's already lied down and stood up a few times, so there isn't much time. She's licking my hands now and nuzzling me with her head. We clear the floor and I ask William to bring me some blankets for her. At the same time, he says he will tell everyone what's happening.

"They'd like to come over," he says when he comes back, and I see that several members have left their positions around the shed and moved in with the goats near where the wall used to stand.

The sky is tilting toward lightness. In the distance, a thin line of sun fires along the outline of a mountain. This is when I see her. Next to Greta and in front of Hal. My mother. Walking straight toward me. I don't have time to react, to stand up, to do anything. I can only watch her as she steps around Tom and around Lilah. She is limping, deeply— and then she is beside me.

"A person has to make these kinds of choices," she says. She's looking at me, but her hand darts down to touch the goat's muzzle.

I look down to the goat but I'm really looking at her hands. The long slender fingers. The rounded knuckles and slightly wrinkled skin. I could be looking at my own hands. Just older. I take a breath. "What kind of choices?" I cannot seem to look at her directly.

"I just knew it. I've always known it." She kneels beside me. It takes her a long time but she doesn't appear to need any help. There's a pause and then, "Oh, neat," she says brightly, pulling her hands away from the goat. "She's started to talk."

"Yes," I say. "For about twenty minutes now."

"Talking" is what goats do when they're about to give birth. They keep their heads angled toward their flanks, make soft noises to their bellies, and nudge the skin.

"She's had quite a shock," I say, just to have something to say.

Her face tenses with the thought. "Isaac will have to rebuild everything. Someone must have sold him bad wood."

I think how this may be true, how it might not be true at all.

The goat's belly is completely still, so I know the kids are lining up to enter the birth canal. The goat lies down and it won't be long now at all.

"Look," she says.

So I look at my mother. I finally look up at her face.

"I couldn't keep you both safe. I told him. It would take too much of me."

"You couldn't?"

"I had to choose." She's shaking her head beneath a knitted wool cap. It's the most exquisite shade of purple. The cap doesn't cover her ears entirely, and I see it—the flesh-colored piece of plastic in her left ear. Her face is both familiar and wholly unknown. It has the same shape, but it's her eyes. Her eyes are all wrong. I don't remember that her eyes were anything like this.

Her hands clutch at threads extending from the cuffs of her winter coat. "Something has happened," she says. "Something has happened or you wouldn't be here."

I nod, and I know as I do that from now on there is this one thing she has gotten perfectly right. Her farfetched conclusion at this instant is the right one.

"That was our deal," she says. "We agreed." Her voice is very anxious. "I promised, you know. He made me promise to let you be. But now you're here."

"I'm here."

"Well, I knew I couldn't keep you both safe."

Eye to eye. We hold it. Our faces nearly touching. This is when I know for sure. I am not her. I will never be her.

"I'm safe," I tell her.

She nods, lets out a breath. "It's been a lot of hard work."

The doe shifts, cries out. I smooth the blanket we've placed under her. My mother reaches out and touches the top of my head. Just once.

"Look," I say, and this time she looks where I have pointed. "She's nearly ready," I say.

"She is," my mother says.

And we watch the little doe as she bleats and pushes, and there in the bright morning light is the first crowning of her baby's head, so perfect and soft and alive.

33

WHEN WAVES REACH A CERTAIN HEIGHT, the only thing to do is match the speed of the boat with the speed of the waves. This means slowing down, not speeding up.

In other words, if I do what I've been taught to do, there's a chance we won't heel or broach. All these years I thought I was preventing a capsize risk, but really I was just risking a broach. On the upside, broaching feels at first like a wild ride, a sublime rollercoaster, until the boat speeds down the other side of the wave crest and slams into the base of the next one. No one can predict what the bow will do when it buries itself into that second wave. The whole boat veers. Tilts.

She gave us gifts.

I will have to go home from *Friends' Farm* and give gifts, too. Maybe Neil will let me. Maybe they'll be enough.

The first will be a promise. "I got it all wrong," I will have to say. "I forgot to look with my own eyes, and so the danger wasn't where I thought it was."

Maybe he'll still be angry, which will mean he hasn't given up. So maybe he will listen.

"I would trade," I will tell him. If I close my eyes we will be at the breakfast table. Two placemats, two plates, both napkins.

"I would trade," I will say again. "I will trade fear, this time, for honesty. I will listen and hope."

If I close my eyes, Neil's gifts will still be somewhere in the house: the petrified wood, the snakeskin and seashells, those cedar pine cones, the agates and fossils.

"I will answer all your questions," I'll have to say, and I will mean it this time.

If I close my eyes, we will be in our house. We will be sad but growing less sad. We will both know how to furl the sails. And between us will sit the possibility of those long toes, that deep voice. Those little hands and smooth shoulders, the dip where the baby's spine curves into a neck.

I will say that I was wrong. That I mistook imagination for delusion, that I made bargains I didn't understand, that I took myself for an owl and flew too often at night and alone. "I cannot really see in the dark," I will say.

And so maybe we could stand perfectly still. We could hold and we could breathe. We could try this all over again. Sail into the waters of our choice. And maybe Neil might listen to me when I explain and show him about the light that attaches to the top mast of a boat, the light that must be turned on when a boat is moored between sunset and sunrise. Because every sailor knows that once that vessel is successfully docked, once the anchor touches the seabed and holds with its weight, it's the anchor light that prevents further collisions, that says *here we are, we're docked, we're at home.*

ACKNOWLEDGEMENTS

A first enormous and heartfelt thank you to my agent Katie Grimm for your tireless support, keen editorial eye, and well-timed pep talks. I appreciate the many hats you wear and your boundless expertise. I'm also very grateful to Robert Lasner and Elizabeth Clementson of Ig for your interest and support. It's a pleasure to work with you and to be in such fine company in your catalog.

Writing would be lonely without such excellent writing and reading friends, so I am very grateful for Alison Anderson, Jennifer Bew Orr, Elizabeth Coleman, Tasja Dorkofikis, Carla Drysdale, Nancy Freund, Steve Himmer, Lou Hundt, the ever-wonderful WH, Catherine Kapphahn, Jen Kerwin, Sophie Knight, Anne Korkeakivi, Patti Marxsen, Karen McDermott, the tall-tale-telling CM, Camala Projansky, and Rodrigo S.M.

I am incredibly thankful for the incomparable VSs—Jason Donald, Jo Ann Hansen Rasch, and valiant bookseller and writer Matthew Wake—for your laughter and friendship, excellent advice, and endless support.

To my dearest L'ATELIERs, Sara Johnson Allen and Laura McCune Poplin, I would not have written the first draft of this book without our writing group so many years ago, nor would I have finished it without your friendship and support at Villeferry for three years. I cannot thank you enough. And I'm so grateful to everyone at L'ATELIER who makes this life of writing both fun and meaningful: Alison Anderson (merci deux fois), Steven Antalics, Edna Ball Axelrod, Angi Dilkes, Carol-Ann Farkas, Nancy Freund (you deserve years of acknowledgements, my friend), Jo Ann Hansen Rasch (again!), Sandra Ionescu, Áine Lorie, Caitlin McGillicuddy, Jen McInerney, Nadu Ologoudou, Pauline Vangheluwen-Blatt, Jo Varnish, and Gabrielle Yetter.

And finally, to my wonderful family and friends, I appreciate your love and support more than I can adequately express: Jennifer Jones Barbour and Josh Barbour, the most amazing Henry and Hazel, Mitch and Mary Jones, Kim and Adam and Mirabelle Bamberg, Jeffrey Coleron and Rhiannon Kruse, Andrée Bailat, and, last but never least, Claude and the marvelous, incredible Emiline—thank you for all that you do and all that you are.